Surprise Surprise

A Psychological Thriller

TANISHA STEWART

Table of Contents

Dear Reader,

Welcome to the fifth installment of The Quiet Ones series. I've always wanted to write a psychological thriller, but I was searching for a source of inspiration. It finally came when Ebony Evans, founder of the EyeCU Reading & Chatting group on Facebook presented a group of authors with a challenge that she calls **Freestyle Fridays**.

In the challenge, the authors were given a theme and a set of pictures and told to let their creative juices flow. From this challenge, Shatina's story was born. You met Shatina in **Should Have Thought Twice**, but the plot gets deeper in *Surprise Surprise*.

Buckle up and enjoy the ride. When you finish, I would love it if you could leave a **rating** or **review**. Happy reading!

Tanisha Stewart

Surprise Surprise

A Psychological Thriller

Chapter 1

Shatina sat frozen in place as Brighton Miller continued his speech. His sinister smile grew more by the second. He continued to walk around the chair that Shatina's twin sister, Shatara, was tied to, glancing down at her, then up at the camera as he traveled. "I bet you're wondering how I found out who you were, Miss Shatina." He paused. "I won't bore you with those minor details, but let's just say I have my sources."

Shatina saw Sam's face redden out of the corner of her eye.

It didn't take a rocket scientist to figure that one out, plus Sam had already admitted sending the footage to the chief of police. *Wait - which footage did she send?* Not that it mattered, since her and Max's identities were revealed anyway, but what exactly did Sam send? The video of Shatina standing over Rodney's body with the gun, or something else? Her eyes shot to Sam. She wanted to ask at that moment, but Brighton was still speaking. His eyes bore into hers and although she knew he couldn't see her, it felt like he could.

All Shatina saw was evil. How could such a man be running for government office? She learned in her dark psychology class that people from all walks of life could exhibit maladaptive traits, but to read about it and to see it were two different things. If successful, this man would be controlling the city Shatina lived in. She'd never given much thought to voting and being active in her community before this moment, but now, she was understanding the weight and implications of her previous inactivity.

"Anywho," Brighton interrupted Shatina's thoughts. "I have a simple request. Turn yourselves into the police so I can get this case off my back, and your sister will be returned to you in the condition I took her." He chuckled. "See, Shatina?" He pointed at himself. "I'm a reasonable man. After all, it's only right that the one who originally pulled the trigger take the fall. I don't know which of you did it, but I do know that you and Max were there before I got to that building. Even if I hadn't arrived, the poor young man would still be dead. This is all on you. You have until the end of the month."

The video faded to black.

There it was. Brighton was giving them an ultimatum. Either face life in prison for murdering Rodney, or never see her sister again.

Shatina didn't know how to feel.

"We'll get her back," Max said softly. He gently rubbed Shatina's hand.

Buster and Sam wore solemn expressions.

Shatina felt the weight of the world on her shoulders, but this situation wasn't entirely her fault. She'd done her dirt, and Max had too, but Sam had reneged on her promise not to release that footage. Shatina studied her, wondering if she felt any genuine remorse for what her selfish actions had caused.

Sam's expression changed from solemn, to guilty, to hopeful. "I have a plan," she announced.

How could she have a plan so quickly? The video had ended barely five minutes ago. Was it Sam's callous nature that allowed her to detach from the weight of the situation fast enough to develop a full plan in five minutes?

Or was there more to the story? What was Sam's real angle? A thought flashed through Shatina's mind: Maybe Sam was in cahoots with Brighton Miller after all.

Shatina contemplated that possibility for a few moments before deciding that didn't make sense. Previously, when Sam had been successful at catching Max and Shatina in her schemes, she couldn't wait to gloat about it, then peel off in her jeep. The Sam standing before her held a different demeanor.

Shatina's shoulders relaxed. Now wasn't the time to point fingers. She needed her sister back.

Shatina shared a glance with Max, then Buster before responding. "I'm all ears."

***

Max and Shatina were still holding hands as they left Sam's cabin. Max couldn't imagine what Shatina was going through, but he wanted her to know that he was with her. Not because he was wrapped up in the situation too, but because he wanted to be there for her.

He couldn't help but to want to take full responsibility for everything they were facing. Although it wouldn't change their circumstances, he had to get it off his chest. He turned to Shatina, gently squeezing her hand before speaking.

"Shatina, I just want to say I'm sorry. If I hadn't gone after Brighton..."

Shatina let his hand go and signaled for him to stop.

"Max, you don't have to apologize to me. I feel just as guilty for my part in this, along with allowing my sister to be blindsided." Tears filled her eyes.

"Blindsided how?" Max stared down at her.

Shatina shook off her emotions. "She kept asking me what was going on, trying to get me to open up. If I hadn't been so stupid..."

He reached out and touched her elbow. "Hey. You were trying to protect her. If she had gotten involved..."

Shatina snorted, cutting him off. "Was I really protecting her though, or just being selfish? I lied to her repeatedly. If I would have opened up, maybe she would have been able to see Brighton coming before he got her. She would have at least been aware of the danger."

Max couldn't argue against that point, but he still disagreed with the idea of Shatina being so hard on herself.

"Babe, we all got wrapped up in a situation we couldn't handle. Yes, we did wrong that led to it, but remember: Brighton is the criminal here. You shot Rodney out of self defense, and you only wanted to go after him to avenge your fiancé's murder. Brighton made the shot that killed him, not you. And Brighton is the one who kidnapped your sister. You've never done anything like that before."

He saw a glimmer of hope in her eyes before it shifted back to guilt. "I've done worse to Shatara before Brighton ever touched her, and now..."

"Yeah, but..." Max saw that trying to defend Shatina against her own guilt was a fruitless endeavor. For every argument he supplied to show that she didn't deserve what was happening to her, she would provide a reason why she did, and the reasons she provided would hold some level of validity.

As if Shatina was reading his thoughts, she said, "You do dirty deeds, you reap the same type of consequences. We don't get to pick how our actions affect us; we just choose how we move."

The weight of her words hit him in more ways than one, and it caused Max to think about his own choices in life. There were many times where he could have gone the right way but chose the wrong one.

Now look where he was.

"Where are you going from here?" he asked, redirecting the subject.

Shatina shrugged. "Home, I guess. I was in the middle of homework before I got the delivery. I don't think I'll be able to focus on much now."

"How about I come over?" he offered. "I could spend the night and help you take your mind off things."

Finally, the deep depression began to recede from her features. Max's heart fluttered at the thought that he caused such a change by his gesture.

"Thanks, Max. I would really appreciate that."

He smiled. "Cool. Let me go grab some things from home and I'll be there soon."

They parted ways to their individual vehicles, and before Max slid into his driver's seat, he caught Sam staring in his direction.

***

When Max entered his apartment, Jared was sitting on the couch, bending to slide on his Timberlands. He looked up to greet Max. "Hey, big bro."

"Hey." Max headed toward his room.

"Yo," Jared called out, causing him to stop in his tracks.

He turned. "What is it?"

Jared waited a beat before responding. "I have some good news for us."

Max wasn't sure he liked the sound of this. "What kind of good news?" Tension filled his body, as if things weren't already stressful enough. Max was almost a hundred percent sure that whatever Jared deemed as *good news* wouldn't be good news at all.

Jared cracked a smile. "I finally got a hit on those guys we were looking for."

Silence filled the room, but expletives filled Max's mind. How was he going to explain to his brother that he was caught up in the moment when he agreed to kill the men who stabbed him? Still, he knew Jared was counting on him not to renege. Besides, he might need more target practice dealing with the likes of Brighton Miller.

"You do?" he finally answered. "Where are they?"

Jared stood, his demeanor giddy, like a kid about to go to Disney World. "I know where they're at right now. We could go do that, then pick up a pizza and some beers and chill after."

Max's fake smile dropped. "Oh... I was supposed to go to my girl's house."

Jared wrinkled his nose. "Your girl? What girl… the one who broke the window?" He gestured toward the recently fixed pane of glass for emphasis.

Max shook his head. "No, that was my ex."

Jared's grin returned as he reached out to dap Max up. "Okay, big bro! I see you! You got these chicks on rotation. I was worried about you for a second, but now I understand you don't need my assistance. So what's up? She got a sister?"

Max didn't know which of Jared's comments to address first, so he decided to redirect. "She does have a sister, and I had planned to introduce you guys soon, but right now she's going through some things. I was going to her house to help calm her down."

Jared nodded. "Oh, I see. Well I won't hold you too long. If we get these guys now, you can go to her afterward and I'll just hit up some hoodrats or something."

Max opened his mouth, then shut it. Jared wasn't following the message he was trying to send. He wanted to just come out and say, *I'm not going*, but he didn't want to offend his brother. Him and Jared had just come to a cordial arrangement. Max didn't want to be back on his bad side. He blew out a breath.

"Okay, let me grab some things from my room and we can go."

Jared was ecstatic. He clapped Max on the back. "Perfect! Let's do this!"

Chapter 2

Shatara had no idea how long it had been since the night she was grabbed from behind and thrust into the back of a van with a potato sack shoved over her head.

She'd attempted to kick and scream, but duct tape silenced her cries, and heavy ropes wrenched her wrists and ankles together.

The ride had been bumpy, but it hadn't taken long. This let her know she was still in town, at least for the time being. When she was taken out of the van to enter the abandoned building, she caught a glimpse of a church with red doors through a hole in the potato sack. Shatara had been trying to place which street the church was on since that moment. She recognized the man who kidnapped her when he started recording the video where he confronted her sister. How was Shatina connected to Brighton Miller? Brighton had mentioned someone being killed and alluded to the fact that Shatina or Max was the killer.

What the hell was Shatina into?

She knew her sister was capable of harming someone - Shatina had almost poisoned her to death after she found out Shatara was sleeping with her first boyfriend, Chris.

But murder though? Why? And how?

A chill ran down Shatara's spine as she remembered how Shatina and Max were originally connected to one another. There was a girl Max planned to kidnap and murder, and he forced Shatina to help him.

Was it forced, though? Shatara originally would have never believed her sister could be in on such a thing, but here we were with another murder.

Who was she related to?

Growing up, Shatina was always the shy, quiet girl with low self esteem. She was bullied endlessly for her weight, looks, and everything else their peers could think of. Shatara noticed, and stepped in to help a few times, but she couldn't be there for every instance, and though it was painful, she had to admit the help she provided wasn't nearly as much as it could have been.

Her mind went to the voice. Shatina had written about hearing a voice that told her to do things in her diary. When Shatara first learned about it, she saw it as a coping mechanism for her sister due to all the hurt she faced. Now she wasn't so sure.

What if Shatina wasn't who Shatara thought she was all along? Clearly, there were some things her sister had been hiding that caused Brighton Miller to kidnap one of her family members.

Shatara wasn't the brightest bulb in the box, but she...

Footsteps were approaching. She straightened in her seat, then braced herself as Brighton Miller entered the dark room where Shatara was tied to a chair.

The first night, she begged for a bathroom, but no one lifted a finger to untie her, and she peed on herself. Shatara had never been more humiliated in her life.

Then, when they finally let her take a shower and gave her clean clothes, she was paranoid, praying they didn't have cameras watching her undress and use the bathroom.

Apart from knowing she was in an abandoned building across from a church, Shatara didn't know much else about her location. She mostly sat in silence, but sometimes she could hear the faint sounds of cars passing by.

Brighton Miller smiled.

"Howdy, sunshine!"

Shatara didn't know how to take him. She knew he didn't have pure intentions for her, judging from how she got here as well as the way he eyed her, but still. She wondered if there was a way to crack him, to persuade him to let her go.

Brighton's smile faltered slightly when she didn't answer. "Not in the mood, huh?"

She opened her mouth to respond, but they were interrupted by two burly men. One of them looked familiar, and Shatara almost blurted that she recognized him, but kept her mouth shut. Who knew what they would do if she started naming names?

The man she recognized, Ate, handed Brighton a McDonald's bag. "Tony forgot the drink," he said, gesturing toward the other guy.

Shatara stared at Ate, wondering if he recognized her as well. Memories were coming back to her. From what she knew about him, Ate earned his nickname because of his large size as well as the fact that he was a known brawler for Blue Street, one of the biggest gangs in the city.

Her heart dropped. If Ate was affiliated with Blue Street, and Brighton was involved with him...

Brighton turned to her, interrupting her thoughts. "Did you hear that, sunshine? These idiots forgot your drink!"

Ate licked his lips in Shatara's direction. "I don't mind going back out to get her one."

"Go ahead, then," Brighton gestured. "Take Tony with you."

They left.

Brighton snapped his fingers, and a young woman came through from the direction Ate and Tony just left. She looked scared, and Shatara didn't like the vibe she was giving off. Her eyes were shifty, like she was ready to jump any minute. Who was this girl, and why did Brighton call her in here?

Brighton gestured at the girl as he spoke. "Sunshine, this is Esmeralda. She's going to help you with your meal."

"Help me...?" Shatara stammered as she spoke.

Brighton cleared his throat before speaking again. "Tony mentioned that you were looking a little froggish when we let you feed yourself."

Shatara's mouth grew dry. Had she been that obvious?

The last time someone came to feed her, she was untied for the duration of the meal. Shatara hadn't made any moves, but she had contemplated throwing the drink in Tony's face and booking it. The only reason she decided against it was because her ankles were still tied to the chair's legs, and she knew there was at least one other person in the building. She had to move smart because she would likely only have one chance.

Now it looked as if she had no chance. If they wouldn't even untie her to let her feed herself, how was she ever going to get out of here?

***

The gun felt like cold steel in Max's hands. He glanced over at Jared, wishing he could tell his brother that he didn't want to complete this mission with him. Shatina had already texted him asking where he was, but Max didn't respond. He didn't want to lie to her, but he certainly couldn't say *committing a few murders with my brother* either.

He swallowed and hoped she wouldn't be too upset with him when he explained.

They got to the street where the guys were congregated in an alley, shooting dice. There were three men there, and one of them looked familiar, but Max couldn't place him.

Jared circled around to the back of the building next to the alley and pulled his ski mask over his head. He cocked his pistol. "Ready, big bro?"

Max swallowed again and nodded, pulling a ski mask over his own head.

Jared kept the car running, which Max saw as both a good and bad idea, but he didn't question it. If he was bold enough to kill a man in cold blood, he should be bold enough to have the getaway car prepared.

Jared went first, creeping around the side of the building. He peeked first, then turned back to Max and nodded.

The men had their backs to them, so they didn't see them coming.

Jared walked slowly at first, then when it looked like one of them was about to turn around, he shot him in his left temple.

Of course, this caused the others to turn around, and that was when Max recognized the third man. It was Rambo, a guy he purchased a gun from before. Rambo whipped his own gun out, training it on Jared. The other guy looked afraid, like he was about to run.

"Do it, bro!" Jared barked. "Do it now!"

Max snapped out of it and realized that Jared was telling him to shoot the other guy since he couldn't. This was the moment of truth. He raised his gun, training it on the guy's chest like Jared taught him. Did he have the guts to pull the trigger?

"Come on!" Jared yelled, and that startled the other guy into action. He took off running. In a split decision, Max closed his eyes and pulled the trigger.

His gun didn't go off. Another one did.

***

Where was Max?

Shatina had texted him over an hour ago but he never responded. Did he change his mind? It usually never took him this long to write or call back. She hoped nothing happened. Her heart sank as she had a bad feeling. Maybe Brighton Miller had changed his mind and gone after him.

She called his phone next, but it went to voicemail. "Come on, Max!" Shatina eyed her car keys. They were hanging near the front door. Maybe she should stop by his apartment to make sure he was okay.

As she was grabbing her coat, her phone lit up on the kitchen table, and Tamika and Tyonne's faces showed up on the screen. Shatina froze, wondering at first why they were calling, then she remembered that as part of their pact to be *renewed besties*, they promised to have a weekly Facetime conversation. Tonight was the first one.

Shatina's mind grew frantic. What if they asked about Shatara? They undoubtedly would try to call her if they hadn't already. What was Shatina supposed to say?

She had been so caught up in worrying about her sister that she hadn't thought of how to handle her family. People were bound to start asking questions after one too many missed calls. The walls were closing in, but Shatina had to answer. If she didn't, they would definitely think something was up.

"Hey," she answered at the last possible second.

Tyonne spoke up first. "Girl, we thought you were about to stand us up like your sister did."

Shatina faked like she was surprised. "What do you mean, Shatara stood you up?"

"We called her first since it was her idea to do the weekly Facetime, but of course, she didn't answer. Probably with some boy."

Shatina palmed her forehead as if she just remembered something. "Oh, that's right!"

"What?" Tyonne and Tamika said in unison.

"Shatara did tell me one of her professors is already giving her a hard time. They have a three-chapter quiz tomorrow. I'm sorry, I meant to text you guys earlier and tell you. She's probably at the library."

Both of their expressions softened. "Aw, poor baby," Tyonne said. "I'm about to text her now and tell her don't stay up too late."

"I'm sure she won't," Shatina said, then second-guessed herself. She didn't want to sound overly sure about what Shatara was doing in case they pressed for more information.

Tamika sighed. "Ugh, anyway, what's up with you?"

This question caught Shatina off guard since her mind was still focused on covering up Shatara's absence. She switched gears.

"Nothing much. Just doing my own homework. I'm taking a lighter load this semester, but these chapters are boring as ever." She rolled her eyes for dramatic effect. At least that part was true. The chapter she tried to read before finding out about Shatara's kidnapping was boring as could be.

"Tell me about it," Tamika said. "I'll be so glad when we graduate. Y'all applying to grad school?"

The conversation went from there, and Shatina relaxed as it progressed, but she knew in the back of her mind that sooner or later, things wouldn't work out so smoothly.

Chapter 3

Max opened his eyes. He didn't know what to expect, but shock was an understatement when he realized that the gun that had gone off was Rambo's, and that he had shot the other guy who was running.

Max's eyes darted back and forth from Jared to Rambo. What the hell was going on?

Jared flashed Max a crooked smile as he tucked his gun back into his waistband, then dapped Rambo up.

"What's going on?" Max asked. Jared began walking back in the direction of the car, then they heard sirens.

Blood pounded in Max's brain as him, Jared, and Rambo booked it the rest of the way to the running vehicle. Thankfully, it was still there. Jared took the driver's seat, Max hopped in the passenger's seat, and Rambo tumbled into the back. They peeled around a few corners in the downtown area near the shooting, but relaxed once they were out of earshot of the sirens. Jared took his ski mask off, and Max did the same.

"That was wicked!" Jared grinned.

"Jared, what the hell happened back there?" Max turned back to look at Rambo. "And what are you doing here?"

Jared answered both questions at once. "Chill bro, it was just a test. You passed with flying colors."

"What do you mean, a test?"

"We know you ain't no killer, Egg Head," Rambo responded. He lowered his window to spit out the back door. "Your brother just wanted to see if you had heart."

"So you knew my gun would jam? How?"

Jared looked at him like he was stupid, then focused back on the road. "It didn't jam, you idiot. It had no bullets."

Max's jaw dropped. "You sent me on a dummy mission, knowing I had no bullets? What if things went wrong? What if they had guns of their own? Wha..."

Jared cut him off mid-sentence, waving his hand. "Yeah, yeah, shoulda coulda woulda. Don't kill the vibe. We were right there with you. We knew nothing was going to happen, and nothing did. Relax."

"Yo, pull in right there," Rambo said as he pointed at a chicken spot. He patted his pocket for his wallet as Jared obeyed.

Max sat there feeling like a complete fool while Jared and Rambo ordered fried chicken dinners, but he declined. Afterward, Jared dropped Rambo off at some girl's house, then headed back toward Max's apartment.

Every time Max felt like he could let his guard down with his brother, Jared pulled another stunt. How was he supposed to trust him?

"Come on man, spit it out," Jared said, glinting at Max with irritation.

"Jared, I feel like you just set me up."

"No, I set up the guys who stabbed me, not you. Chill. Like I told you, it was a test. Rambo and I..."

"A test for what though? I've never once crossed you, Jared. Not even when we were kids. If anybody needs to be tested, it's you!"

Jared looked shocked. "What the hell is that supposed to mean?"

"What do you think I mean? You're all over the place. One minute we're cool, the next you're trying to kill me. You force me back in the drug game, talking about we're partners, but only pay me sixty dollars. You son me in front of your friends but want to call me *big bro* like you have even an ounce of respect for me. Shall I go on?"

Jared looked like he was taking in Max's words, which was surprising.

"Dang, I didn't think of it like that. Most of the time I'm just jerking your chain, Max. Don't ever doubt my loyalty. If anything ever happened to you, these streets would be full of blood, believe that."

The way he spoke those words without hesitation made Max believe his brother. Jared had been erratic with his behavior, but he had tried multiple times to bond as well. Maybe Max was too hard on him. In fact, maybe Max needed to open his eyes and see the bigger picture.

He turned to his baby brother, seeing him in a whole new light.

"Jared, I have to tell you something."

***

Shatara was beginning to lose hope. Not only was Brighton having Esmeralda hand-feed her like she was an infant, she had to relieve herself and shower with the bathroom door cracked and someone standing right outside of it.

There was no way out. No weapons, no allies, and no plan.

Shatara began to pray that someone would start asking questions about where she was. Had she made the news? Did Shatina call the police? Shatara's gut told her she hadn't. If she did, Brighton would have mentioned it, wouldn't he?

She was tired of sitting in the dark, crying her eyes out, with no company except random rats that ran across the floor periodically, and Esmeralda, who at least smiled at her when they interacted. Now that she thought of it, Shatara wasn't sure if that was a good or bad thing. What if Brighton was having Esmeralda purposefully act friendly to see if Shatara let her guard down? He had asked her a bunch of questions about Shatina, none of which she had answered. Shatara wasn't stupid, nor was she disloyal. She prayed that her sister was doing something to get her out of here. Shatina was her only hope.

Jarring her from her thoughts, Brighton waltzed into the room, holding out a laptop.

"What is this?" Shatara asked, when he placed it on her lap, then gestured for Ate, who entered the room behind him, to untie her.

Brighton smiled. "You're taking a leave of absence from school. I meant to have you do it earlier, but it slipped my mind. I already have the school's site pulled up, so just enter your credentials and fill out the form."

Shatara's heart sank further than she thought possible. She hadn't even considered someone at her school calling the authorities, but now it looked as if that ship would sail too.

She stared at Ate, then something dawned on her.

That was where she was!

She couldn't for the life of her place which street the church with the red doors was on until this moment. She had to find a way to send a message to her sister.

Ate finished untying her, and as soon as her fingertips touched the keys to enter her username and password, Tony walked into the room holding a cell phone. "Boss, it's Toledo."

Brighton stared at him for a few moments, glanced at Shatara, then turned back to Tony. He sucked his teeth. "Alright, I'm coming." He gestured at Ate. "Watch her. Make sure she doesn't do anything stupid."

Ate flashed a smile. "Gotcha."

Shatara wouldn't dare try Ate. He could probably kill her with his bare hands if he wanted.

"Go on, Ma," he said with a smile. "The computer don't bite."

Shatara focused on the screen, her mind racing with how she could send a quick message to her sister without Ate noticing. She knew she had to watch her body language as well as her actions on the computer. If Tony read her facial expression that easily, Ate probably would too. She forced a dull look into her eyes as the site granted her access to her student account. Then, the idea came. When student accounts pulled up, the school's email provider pulled up with it. All she had to do was open an email, send it to Shatina, and pray she checked it. She had to move quickly and inconspicuously though. This was her only chance.

"How long does the form take?" Ate asked, looking like he wanted to snatch the computer. Was he afraid of Brighton or something? Shatara had been on it for less than a minute.

"I'm waiting for the screen to load," she said, and turned it to face him so he could see. Thankfully, the screen was actually loading at that moment, which granted her some credibility, judging from Ate's facial expression. He nodded and relaxed.

The screen popped up for her to submit the form. She contemplated which box to check and decided to play dumb. "Should I put that I'm sick, and that's why I need the leave of absence?"

Ate shrugged. "I have no idea, college girl. Just say something that sounds believable."

"Okay…" Shatara pretended to think as she discreetly pulled up her email provider. She forced herself to not even glance in Ate's direction so as to not let him notice her plan.

She typed two quick words to Shatina, clicked send, then pressed the red box to exit the email just as Ate walked over and stared at the screen to see what she was doing.

"What were you just typing?" he asked, staring with suspicion.

"They asked for a further explanation," she said, pointing at the box below the option she checked. Thankfully, she had already typed a few words into the box before he walked over, so it made her story seem believable. Ate watched as she typed a paragraph about being sick and having family issues, so she needed a few weeks off, possibly the whole semester. She clicked Send, then stared up at him, praying internally that he wasn't tech savvy enough to try to figure out if she had done anything else.

He didn't.

He took the laptop, placed it on the floor, and re-tied her wrists to the chair. "Good girl," he said, patting her head like a dog before exiting the room to bring the laptop back to Brighton.

***

Sam's mind had been going haywire lately, for more reasons than one. Max and Shatina were on the verge of going to prison, not to mention whatever Brighton had planned for Shatina's sister if they didn't turn themselves in or the crew's plan didn't work.

On top of that, her relationship with Robert was shaky, and it would only get worse if he found out she was the reason he had to visit his newly reunited son behind prison walls.

Sam's usual response to being the cause of other people's misfortune was to cackle and give herself a pat on the back for a job well done. Not this time. This time, she was hurting people she cared about.

Robert made Sam feel for him in ways she never had for another man, and although she enjoyed wreaking havoc on Max and Shatina's lives, she'd grown fond of them.

In a morbid way, they were her only friends.

Of course, Max and Shatina would never describe their relationship as a friendship, but still...

"You're spacing out again," Robert said, and Sam snapped out of it.

She was supposed to be focusing on the conversation, and it was an important one. Robert was going to tell her if he wanted to move forward with her, or if he was ready to cut his losses after her fight with Lacey.

Sam had a hunch that he still wanted to be with her - otherwise, why would he ask her to dinner instead of just meeting at one of their houses?

"I'm sorry. Just a lot on my mind."

Robert's brows wrinkled. "What's going on?"

Sam shook her head. "Just life, and then the situation with you and me."

"What's going on with life?"

"Nothing. I can handle it."

"Sam, if you can't open up to me about what's going on, how do you expect us to be together?"

"Didn't you call this meeting to let me know if you were breaking up with me?"

Robert gave her a look. "Don't play that game. You knew when I asked you to meet me at this restaurant that I wasn't breaking up with you. Don't act like you're over there holding your breath."

He was right, but Sam certainly couldn't tell him what was going on. Instead, she cracked a smile. It was genuine, and she hoped it hid her underlying emotions. "Glad to hear that you're not going to let my little mishap ruin what we have."

As was customary for him, Robert had to have the last word. "As long as you don't refuse to let me in, and cause what we have to become what we had."

Chapter 4

ax finally knocked on Shatina's door, hours after the time he said he was coming. Shatina was livid to say the least. She'd already eaten but didn't bother to put a plate up for him. The food was in a pot in the fridge, but still. How dare he stand her up at a time like this?

Shatina left him standing at the door when she opened it without a word.

"Shatina..." he started, closing and locking the door as she plopped down on the couch.

"Go on, Max. I'm dying to hear what was more important to you than being here for me."

"Babe, I swear, it's not like that. Look..." His voice trailed off.

He took a few moments too long to answer, so Shatina glared up at him. "Well?"

He spoke slowly. "I had to help Jared with some things."

"Help Jared with what things?" Shatina straightened in her seat. Whatever it was, it couldn't be good. From everything Max had shared about his brother so far, Shatina knew he was bad news.

Max swallowed. "He wanted me to help him get the guys who stabbed him."

Shatina stared at him. "Get them how?"

Max didn't answer.

Shatina's head snapped backward in shock. "Are you kidding me? Do we not already have a murder charge over our heads? What the hell is wrong with you, Max?" Without realizing it, Shatina's voice had risen to dangerous levels. She prayed none of her neighbors heard what she just said.

Max held his hands up. "I swear, I didn't pull the trigger. I…"

"That doesn't matter, Max, and you know it! You were there, so you're still culpable."

They stared at each other. Shatina didn't know what to think or do.

"There's more," Max said before dropping his head like he was guilty.

Shatina crossed her arms. "What else is it, Max?" Her eyes narrowed.

"I asked him to help us."

No, he didn't. No, Max did not ask his sociopathic, reckless and dangerous brother to help with their plan.

Shatina had no more words.

"Babe…" Max started, but she was already walking toward her bedroom, slamming the door behind her.

***

Sam had just finished texting Buster, asking for an update on the plan when Brighton called her phone. As much as she didn't want to answer, she knew she had to.

"Hello?"

"Hey, beautiful." Sam could hear the smile in his voice.

"What do you want, Brighton?"

"Is that how you greet the love of your life?"

Sam almost snorted but caught herself. One thing she had been worried about was the possibility that Brighton knew she was working with Max and Shatina against him. If he didn't suspect her, that only worked in their favor.

"*Love of my life* is a stretch, but I guess we're cordial."

Brighton chuckled. "Cordial, huh? You know I owe you one."

Sam's suspicions were confirmed. Brighton didn't have a clue that she was working with Max and Shatina. He still thought she had sent that footage out of love for him, not rage against them. At the time the footage was sent, she had felt something for Brighton, but that was before she met Robert. Now Brighton was nothing more than an annoyance. One she couldn't wait to erase from her life for good.

"I guess you do owe me," she answered in a sultry tone. "How are you going to repay your debt?"

Brighton chuckled again, then lowered his voice an octave to match her flirtatious vibe. "How about an evening under the stars?"

***

Buster texted Sam to give her an update, then re-focused his binoculars on McConnell, who was exiting his office to go home from work.

Buster had been tailing him for the past few days as part of Sam's plan. She had explained to the crew that if they went after Brighton directly, it would be too obvious and their covers would likely be blown. The next best person was McConnell, Brighton's lawyer. McConnell undoubtedly had mountains of dirt on Brighton, so learning his daily routines would allow them to set up a plan to break into his house, possibly find dirt on them both, and either flip McConnell against Brighton, or take whatever they found straight to the police, provided that it was airtight evidence.

Buster hoped this plan worked. He felt bad for what he had forced Max and Shatina to do, despite the cocky way he handled it. It was fun and games at first, but after he received the money, it dawned on him that if they had gotten caught that night at his old job, he could have gotten them locked up for a long time.

He owed it to them to help take Brighton down and save Shatina's sister.

Buster smirked as he had another thought. He couldn't front - he was blown away by the picture he saw of Shatara on her cell phone the day she was kidnapped. He found himself glancing at her social media pictures ever since. Buster had been messing around with Sam for a minute, but she ghosted him once she got with that Robert dude, Max's father. Buster knew he didn't have a leg to stand on with her, so he didn't bother to try.

Shatara was looking right though...

McConnell's vehicle finally began to move.

Buster waited several moments, then pulled a few car lengths behind him.

At the street McConnell usually took a left, this time, he took a right. Buster was intrigued. He followed McConnell down a few side streets, briefly worrying that McConnell had discovered he was being followed, before seeing him stop in front of a bar. Buster sat and waited as

McConnell went in, contemplating whether he should follow him inside.

He pulled out his binoculars again to check out the bar through the windows. It looked pretty crowded, which wasn't out of the ordinary for a Friday night.

Buster thought about it for another second, then decided to go in.

He spotted McConnell immediately, sitting at the bar and already drinking. He watched as McConnell chatted with the bartender, typed something on his phone, then slid it back into his jacket pocket, which was hanging on the back of the stool he was sitting on. This bar was fancy. Usually, the stools at the bars Buster went to didn't have backs on them. Nevertheless, it gave Buster an idea.

He waited a few more moments, hanging out by the jukebox and vibing to the music, ordering a few drinks from a shot girl to blend in with the crowd, and watching McConnell like a hawk out of the corner of his eye.

Another man walked in, greeted McConnell, and sat next to him. The seat on his other side was still empty.

Buster had to time this just right, and he had to move quickly. He sipped on his drink while glancing around the bar. No one seemed to be paying attention to him. They were focused on having a good time.

McConnell was in deep conversation, leaning in to face the other guy he was talking to. This looked like it was about to be easy as hell.

Buster walked with a nonchalant gait, then pulled up a seat next to McConnell. He waited a few more moments before ordering a drink from the bartender, then took in the atmosphere once again to make sure no one was watching. After that, he did a trick he learned from childhood, when he got into mischief with his cousin

Michael. He slipped McConnell's phone from his pocket with ease, confidently entering McConnell's wedding anniversary as the passcode. He'd gotten that information from his wife's social media page. Voila. It worked.

Buster was so full of cockiness at how easy this mission was turning out to be that he didn't notice someone standing directly in front of him.

"Hey," she said.

Buster whipped his head up in fear, then relaxed when he noticed it was the shot girl, holding a flirtatious gaze.

"Hey," he said, licking his lips and relaxing with McConnell's phone as if it were his own. He installed the secret app he had created previously to clone people's phones without having to use the usual channels. He sent himself a text from the app which would contain the link to crack the internal code to McConnell's device. Once that was done, he would be behind McConnell's security walls and could see everything he did. He could even search emails, other apps, text messages, and anything else McConnell's phone had in its storage.

Now all Buster had to do was flirt enough with this shot girl til she left him alone, pray McConnell didn't reach into his jacket pocket any time soon, and get out of the bar before he noticed he was there.

Chapter 5

Shatina tuned out Max's incessant knocking on her bedroom door. He pleaded for her to hear him out and accept his apology, but all she did was turn her music up in response.

Later in the night, her playlist switched to love songs, and she started feeling bad for blocking him out. He was only trying to help, after all. Plus, whatever caused Max to shift in his stance from hating Jared to trusting him had to be huge.

Sucking her teeth, Shatina kicked her comforter off her body, then rose from the bed to talk to Max. When she got to the living room, however, her heart sank. He wasn't there.

He left, the voice told her. *You should have heard him out. You should have...*

Max's voice came from behind, startling her. "Hey."

Shatina calmed her racing heart and answered. "Where did you come from?"

Max pointed. "The bathroom."

"Oh." She hadn't thought to check there.

"You're still upset with me?" he asked, a look of hope in his pupils.

Shatina shook her head. "As long as you believe Jared can truly be trusted."

"He can." Max sounded sure of himself, so Shatina decided to cross it off her list of worries. Couldn't cry over spilled milk now.

They walked over to the couch and sat down.

"I thought you were asleep by now," Max commented.

"Nope. Couldn't."

"Me either."

They sat in silence for a few more moments. "Do you really think we'll get my sister back?" Shatina asked, but at that moment, her playlist switched to a rock and roll station. She rolled her eyes and went to her bedroom to shut off the Bluetooth speaker. When she picked up her phone, she noticed some texts from Buster and an email notification.

She swiped the screen down to see what Buster texted before deciding if his message was worth opening before morning, but her eyes caught the email first. The sender was Shatara!

"Max!" she gasped and raced to the living room to meet him.

"What is it?" he asked, looking bewildered.

"Shatara sent me an email!"

He froze. "What did it say?"

Shatina swiped her screen and opened it, then wrinkled her nose before catching the message. Her heart began pounding harder. "She just told me where she was."

Max stood to stare at the message on her phone.

"*Seth's court?* What does that mean?"

"The basketball court where Seth was shot! This was probably all she had time to type, but I know that's what she meant."

Max wasn't following. "But where exactly is she on that street though? There are multiple apartment buildings on both sides. The street spans at least a mile."

"Let's drive there. I bet we can narrow it down." Shatina went to grab her coat, but Max grabbed her arm.

"Wait, we can't go there without a plan."

"Yes the hell we can! My sister's there. Besides, we're just narrowing down the location, not actually breaking in tonight."

Max took a breath. "Shatina..."

"Max, this is my sister. Do you not understand? If she gave me a lead, I'm following it tonight. With or without you." She continued on her way to her coat.

Max tried one more time to stop her. "We can't take our cars. They'll recognize us."

"Then we'll order an Uber. Let's go."

***

Sam stared at the empty bottle, which largely resembled her empty life. Who did she think she was fooling, plotting and scheming against people, only to lose those closest to her by her own actions?

Granted, her father had crossed her in more ways than she could count, but still. He was the only parent she had, outside of her mother.

Sam thought about reaching out to him many times since the fight with Lacey, but she couldn't bring herself to do it. Not like he reached out to her either. He was probably still honeymooning with that skank. Sam reached for her phone to check on her suspicions. She was right. Dexter and Lacey were having the time of their lives. Kayaking somewhere across the country. They didn't share their location, only pictures. Probably as a precaution against Sam.

Ruining their wedding day might have seemed childish to some, but Sam didn't regret her actions, despite the consequences they caused. Still, she couldn't help but to notice that she was left unfulfilled. Sure, it was exciting to see her plan executed perfectly and to obtain the desired results, but in the grand scheme of things, her actions hadn't amounted to anything.

They were still married, and nothing could change that.

Dexter would likely forget all about her and spend the rest of his life with her ex best friend. Sam was disgusted by the thought, then her mind traveled to the fact that she was in a serious relationship with Robert. Looking at it from that angle, she was no better than Lacey, despite the fact that she hadn't set out to date her ex's father intentionally.

On second thought, forget that. Her and Lacey's actions couldn't even be compared. Not only had Lacey schemed on Max while him and Sam were together, she married Sam's father! Sam allowed herself to retain a sense of dignity despite the darkness of her actions. She may have been a number of things, but she had never been disloyal to someone she valued.

Had Lacey ever valued her? It seemed that she had while growing up, but now Sam wasn't so sure. Lacey didn't have a problem pushing up on her boyfriend or father... Maybe she secretly disliked Sam all along.

Whatever. I hope their boat tips over.

Sam was done lamenting for the night. She picked up the empty bottle, trudged to her kitchen to throw it in the trash, then went back to her room to try to get some sleep.

Tomorrow was her date with Brighton.

***

Buster scrolled through the various apps on McConnell's phone, bored out of his mind. From the looks of it so far, the only thing the man did for excitement was play Solitaire. No dirt to be found.

Buster was about to give up and sift through McConnell's emails, when he spotted an icon he didn't recognize. Clicking it, his heart leapt.

"Now we're cooking!"

A smile grew across Buster's face.

Chapter 6

The Uber was ten minutes away and largely overpriced since it was a surge time. Shatina was convinced that they were about to find her sister, but Max wasn't so sure. He didn't like the idea of going down that street in the middle of the night, especially since it was a gang-populated area. Granted, he'd sold drugs there plenty of times, but the middle of the night on a weekend? Anything could pop off. Heck, Seth had gotten shot in the head in broad daylight at the basketball court!

Still, he couldn't let Shatina go there alone. Perhaps he was reluctant because his mind was still spinning over Jared. Jared might have thought that killing two men in cold blood was a walk in the park, but Max didn't see it that way. All he saw were bodies piling up, and he was much too close in association with them all. Max still wasn't fully over Rodney's death, despite the fact that the man died after trying to kill him.

Maybe Max just didn't like the concept of death. It was so final. Once it was done, there was no turning back for either side. Once you had a body over your head, it was there for life...

"Finally!" Shatina huffed, her soft breath forming a circle in the cold night air. She led the way to the Uber, but Max held the door open for her and they slid inside.

They greeted the driver but shared a glance to keep their conversation to a minimum. "Blue Street, huh?" the driver commented. "I've dropped a few people off in that area tonight. Must be a party."

Max and Shatina didn't answer, though Max was now worried that his suspicions were confirmed about this being a bad idea.

Traffic was congested in some areas, but they made it to their destination without incident.

Max and Shatina walked quietly, not sure what they were looking for, but hoping to find Shatara's location all the same.

Max stopped short as a thought occurred to him. Chills went down his spine. "Shatina, what if they..." He was going to say, what if they had someone looking out for them, since Brighton had her sister, but Shatina was already pointing and talking.

"That has to be it!" she hissed. She was pointing at an abandoned building across from the church they were standing in front of.

Max kept his emotions in check, though his eyes darted back and forth before responding. He prayed they weren't being watched. "What makes you so sure?"

"It's the only abandoned building on the street. The most inconspicuous place."

Max opened his mouth to protest but thought about it. Shatina might have been right. He was originally thinking they had Shatara in one of the apartment buildings, which was where most of his fear came from. No way was he waltzing into a building controlled by the

Blue Street gang in the middle of the night asking about a missing woman. Him and Shatina would be lucky to finish their sentence, much less leave with their lives.

Max relaxed slightly, though his head was still on a swivel. He could tell Shatina wanted to cross the street and investigate, despite her earlier promise that they were only going to narrow down a location.

He got it - this was her sister. Emotions were high, and they had no idea what Brighton could be doing to her in there. In the video, Shatara looked fine, despite her tears, but she had been with Brighton for at least a few days by now.

Shatina was staring at him, asking for an okay.

Max nodded, and they walked until they were past the building, then crossed the street to circle back.

***

Despite the chilly temperatures, Shatina's body was pumping with adrenaline. She prayed that she was right about her sister being in this building.

When her and Max approached, the hairs on the back of her neck stood up. She pointed at the dirt driveway, which was misted with frost. "Look."

There were tire tracks. Someone had been here. That thought caused Shatina's heart to sink. Had they moved her sister?

"That doesn't necessarily mean anything," Max said in a low voice. "It could have been someone making a U-turn."

Shatina was already on the move.

"Hey!" Max hissed, but she was too far gone. Before she knew it, she was rattling a side door to see if it was unlocked. It took a few rough pulls, but it opened.

Shatina turned back to Max. He looked pissed that she was going this far, despite what they agreed to, but he nodded. "Go ahead."

They crept into the building, which of course, was empty.

Max shut the door behind them, which Shatina thought was a good idea. They didn't want anyone possibly coming back, seeing the door open, and ambushing them.

"She's here, I know it," Shatina whispered, but her heart was filled with anguish. It didn't seem like she was. There were no sounds except the dripping of water.

Wait - dripping water? Why would there be dripping water in an abandoned building? Of course, there were a number of reasons that could be provided, but Shatina was on the move. She strained to hear the source of the water, going from room to room in what used to be an office building.

Finally, they stumbled upon a room that had a bathroom in it.

Foot tracks were all over the dusty floor. Shatina was right. Someone had been here, but they weren't here any longer.

She closed her eyes to envision the room Shatara was in during the video. This had to be the same room.

Shatina walked over to the bathroom, where the shower head was dripping water. There was also a space heater on the other side of the room, indicating that someone had used it to heat the room recently.

Her sister had been here, she knew it. She just needed a clue to...

Her foot crunched over something on the ground.

Shatina moved her foot back, then whipped out her cell phone to shine the flashlight on what she had just stepped on.

Waves of emotion ran through her.

"What is it?" Max asked, and Shatina bent down to pick up the remnants of the acrylic nail tip, the same color and design Shatara chose while they got manis and pedis at Disney World.

"She was here," Shatina croaked, feeling like someone just punched a hole in her chest.

"What is that?" Max asked. "How do you know it's hers?"

"It's hers, Max." Shatina sniffled. "But now she's gone, and I don't know where they've taken her."

***

The next day, Max and Shatina headed to the cabin for a debriefing with Buster and Sam. Buster said he had some new intel on McConnell, and Shatina wanted to talk about what they found at the warehouse.

Max felt for his woman.

She couldn't stop crying the night before, despite Max's attempts to reassure her. She had gone back to blaming herself for not finding Shatara in time.

"Max, she sent me that email hours prior! If I had just been checking my phone..."

"Shatina, why would you think to check your emails? You had no way of knowing she would reach out to you. Besides, if we went there when she sent the message, it could have been dangerous. We had no plan, and we have no idea how many people are working with Brighton. Babe, we're gonna find her. Don't lose hope."

That seemed to calm her for ten minutes, before she started bawling again. Max held her in his arms until she fell asleep.

When they entered the cabin, Buster and Sam were already there.

Sam saw the look on Shatina's face and rushed over to hug her. It happened so fast, Shatina hugged her back, but when they pulled away from each other, they both wore the same confused expression.

"Thanks," Shatina said, breaking the awkward silence.

Sam nodded, now looking more embarrassed than confused.

Buster and Max shared a glance as well. Buster's brow was raised, but Max shook his head to tell him to let it go. No need to crack a joke at a time like this.

Max cleared his throat. "Buster, what did you find?"

Buster snapped his focus away from Sam and Shatina. "Oh - yeah, this is good." He pulled up a chair at the table as they all walked over to sit.

"Turns out McConnell's not as squeaky clean as I thought he was."

Shatina wore a sullen look. "Go on."

Buster's excitement slightly dwindled, but he pressed on. "He's part of a sex club."

Sam wrinkled her nose. "A sex club? Ew, who would want him?"

Buster's smirk returned. "It's not that kind of party. They wear masks so no one knows their identity, then they have a bunch of rooms. If someone gives you the nod, they are agreeing to go into a room with you to fulfill your sexual fantasy."

Everyone stared at Buster as he continued.

"Turns out, McConnell is a Tripsolagniac."

Max blinked. "A what?"

"He gets turned on by having his hair shampooed."

Sam scrunched her face. "That's a thing?"

Buster nodded. "Apparently. He has tons of messages dating back for the past six years. He visits the club at least once a month to get his desires fulfilled, but he's terribly ashamed of his fetish, which is why he doesn't just have his wife do it. Even though he doesn't have sex with the women who shampoo his hair, he forms emotional bonds with them through the app. He seems to have a pattern of becoming obsessed with them until they curve and block him for good."

"That's... interesting," Sam commented.

"So, who's up for a visit to the club?" Buster asked, staring at no one but Sam.

Sam pointed at herself. "Me?"

"Well, Shatina can't do it."

"I can't do it either! He'll recognize me just like he would recognize her!"

Buster sighed. "Sam, you know how to finesse a man like no other." His eyes shot to Shatina. "No offense. Plus, remember, you're wearing a mask."

Sam rolled her eyes. "Whatever. I'll do it, but how exactly is this going to help move the plan along?"

When Max and Shatina left the cabin, Shatina seemed to be in better spirits.

"We're one step closer," Max offered, to test the waters.

Shatina nodded. "I just hope it works."

They headed back to her apartment and warmed up some leftovers from the night prior. After their meal, Shatina said she wanted to go to bed. Max didn't want to press her, so he let her go to her room and turned on the TV to catch up on one of his shows before drifting off himself.

Unfortunately, his night was far from over.

A Breaking News signal flashed on the screen, and Max's heart dropped at the sight of a reporter standing in front of the alley where Jared and Rambo shot those guys.

"A new development has arisen in this ongoing investigation of a cold-blooded double homicide in the alley behind me," the reporter said in a neutral tone.

"Police have mentioned that there was a witness to the crime. They are questioning him as we speak, but more details will be offered when we receive them. Such a sad day for our city, with the murder rate on the rise since..."

Max couldn't process the rest of her words. There was a witness? He hadn't seen anyone in the alley. He frantically grabbed his phone, scouring all the local news sites to see if any others had mentioned who the witness might be, or what he said he saw.

"I knew I shouldn't have done that!"

Chapter 7

Thanks to Buster's fake ID skills, a new wig, and some stilettos, Sam had been transformed into a different woman. Her mask covered most of her face. She hoped this plan worked. Buster's idea was to have her give McConnell the nod, take him to one of the rooms, and fulfill his fetish while video recording the incident. Recording was risky business since cell phones weren't allowed on the premises. Sam had to get creative about how to record him. Thankfully, Buster had access to tiny devices that packed a powerful punch. The tiny cameras recorded audio and video, were wireless, and could last for hours. Sam slipped it into her bra, but it was so tiny she barely felt it. She prayed that it wouldn't slip out and fall to the floor from under her dress.

One other thing she was worried about was whether she would be able to pick McConnell out of the crowd with it being a masquerade party. She hoped it wasn't too difficult. Sam handed over her cell phone to one of the doormen, and he sealed it in a clear pouch with her username from the app etched across the front but gave her the key. Sam thought that was a pretty good system – each pouch had its own unique key, so as long as she didn't lose her key, her cell phone could only be returned to her.

Once she got McConnell into one of the rooms, she would send a text to Shatina so Buster and Max could break into his house. How would she send the text? Her other phone. Sam held back a sinister smile as she sauntered past the doorman. The other phone was a throwaway, stashed in a pocket in her panties, so it didn't have a camera. Its sole purpose was to send the signal to the crew or receive one if things went wrong on their end. Sam's nose wrinkled at the thought of panties with pockets. There was literally no purpose, and she told Buster so when he presented them to her. He made a joke about it, and normally Sam would have been weirded out about such a thing, but if Buster was one thing, he was resourceful. Sam shook her head, focusing on the mission at hand. They decided to tackle McConnell from both angles at once in the interest of time and gaining an advantage. Sam hoped they found something, or at least that the recording worked so they could flip McConnell. Otherwise, the crew was fresh out of options. Sam's date with Brighton was a bust. He didn't mention Shatina or Max once. All he did was rave about his plans for the city and the prospects of their relationship in the future. Sam couldn't wait for the day she would tell him that there wasn't any future for them. That ship had sailed. She was with Robert now.

Sam mingled with a few people, striking conversations with some and flirting with others, then she spotted McConnell. It had to be him. His hair color and style distinguished him from the rest of the partygoers. McConnell's hair was almost all white. It was expertly coiffed, and it reached the back of his neck, almost to his shoulders.

Sam took in his height, build, and the way he walked to make sure it was him before she approached.

Their eyes met through their masks, but he didn't seem to recognize her. Sam was wearing green contacts to throw off her appearance even more.

Sam's eyes swept up and down his body as if she were attracted to him.

McConnell's cheeks grew pink on the sides of his mask.

Got him, she thought, as she gracefully nodded in his direction, then gestured toward one of the doors.

McConnell immediately followed her, closing the door behind them.

***

The text came through on Shatina's phone. It was time for Buster and Max to break into McConnell's house. They brought various tools with them in case they were necessary, but Buster was banking on the fact that they had left at least one door or window unlocked.

Him and Max casually crossed the street to the house. No neighbors appeared to be paying attention. Max tried a side door first, but it was locked. Next, they tried a series of windows leading to the back door, which was a sliding glass style.

Buster's suspicions were confirmed. It was unlocked.

"Showtime," he whispered, and him and Max walked inside, sliding it back closed behind them.

***

Shatina hoped this night went smoothly and that both plans yielded results. They needed all the ammunition they could get to either flip McConnell or find information that would lead them to Shatara directly.

"Please let this work," she breathed.

Chapter 8

Buster and Max crept through McConnell's kitchen, hoping he had no pets or cameras set up inside his house. The coast was clear. They traveled through his living room and den, then began opening doors, hoping they would find an office.

"I bet it's that one," Max said, pointing at a door that had a portrait of McConnell's headshot next to it.

Buster chuckled. "Agreed. This guy."

They made their way to the door, and not surprisingly, it was locked.

"Thankfully, we brought tools!" Buster said, then knelt to work on the lock. Less than five minutes later, they were entering McConnell's office, which looked something like a library. Three of the four walls were covered with books. Law manuals, history books, textbooks, and encyclopedias. The place was a gold mine for information. Max hoped the information they were looking for could be found here too.

His mind traveled back to the other day, when he saw the Breaking News signal on television. He reached out to Jared the next morning, his mind frantic.

"Jared, there's a problem. The news said there was a witness!"

The brothers were on Facetime and Max was sitting in his car. He didn't want Shatina worried about this. Apparently, Jared wasn't worried either because he cracked his customary grin.

"Oh, I know all about the witness. Chillax, big bro. I got this."

"What do you mean, you got this?"

"I sent the witness."

"You sent the... why would you do that?"

Jared stared at him as if he had three heads. "To throw the police off our track, duh."

Max sighed. "Who is the witness, Jared? How do you know he can be trusted? Does he know who really did it? And what did he say?"

Jared's eyes lit up like he was enjoying all this. "So many questions, which should I answer first? The witness is Rambo's cousin, so like I said, we're good. He told the police some cock and bull story with believable details, but nothing he said was the truth. They bought it, and they are searching for the fictitious criminals as we speak."

Max was developing a headache. Why on earth did he ever agree to go with Jared that day?

"Max, calm down," Jared said, his expression turning serious. "I said I had you, and I do. Nothing's going to happen."

Max sucked his teeth. "Yeah, I hope it doesn't." He ended the call.

Max snapped out of his memory when he noticed Buster staring at him.

"You good?" Buster asked.

Max nodded.

Buster grinned, then slid on a new pair of gloves, putting the old ones in his pocket. "You wanna watch the door while I hack the computer?"

Max shook his head. "No need to hack. Look." He pointed, and sure enough, McConnell's password was written on a sticky note that was situated in the top middle of his desktop screen.

They shook their heads at each other, then Max went to stand by the door while Buster turned on the computer.

McConnell's password worked. Buster was in.

***

Max and Buster had been inside McConnell's house for less than ten minutes when a vehicle pulled into the driveway, followed by another one.

The color drained from Shatina's face. Buster had said that McConnell's wife texted him saying she was supposed to be working late. Who was this?

A woman emerged from the first vehicle, and a man from the second.

Shatina texted Max and Buster simultaneously. *You've got company!*

McConnell's wife and her guest strode toward the front door.

***

Sam was nervous that she wouldn't be able to pull this off, but she refused to let her emotions show it. "So tell me... what's your fantasy?" she purred in a midwestern accent.

McConnell licked his lips. "I noticed your hands from across the room. Such delicate fingers."

That comment almost threw Sam for a loop, but she stayed in character. She caressed one hand with the other in a slow and seductive fashion. "Oh, do I? Would you like me to touch you with these hands?"

McConnell nodded, then slid a bottle of Head and Shoulders out of his jacket pocket, along with a spray bottle of clear liquid that Sam assumed was water, setting them both on the shiny wooden table.

"What's this about?" Sam said in a playful, but excited tone.

McConnell removed his jacket in a smooth fashion, then slipped off his shoes. "You'll see soon enough. Mind if I make myself comfortable?"

Sam nodded, not taking her eyes off him. "Sure. We'll be here a while, so make yourself right at home."

McConnell smiled with boyish charm, then sat back in a leather chair across from the bed, running his fingers through his locks. "See what I'm doing here?"

"Mm hm."

He looked back at her and drawled, "I've been a dirty boy. I need you to clean me up."

Sam almost burst out laughing, but she refocused and went deeper into character. She sauntered over to him, gently lifting the bottle of Head and Shoulders from the table.

"So Mr. Dirty Boy, would you like a lot of lather, or just a little?"

McConnell loosened his tie and unbuttoned his shirt. "Lather me up, baby."

Sam discreetly slid the throwaway phone from her panty pocket, sent the text, then removed the recording device from her bra, turning on the video camera and aiming it at an angle where McConnell's profile could be seen. She pressed Record.

McConnell had his eyes closed the entire time, so he didn't notice her stealthy movements.

He jerked slightly when she began spraying his head with the water, but he calmed and began breathing deeply the moment her fingers touched his scalp.

"Ooh yeah, right there baby," he moaned.

Sam's fingers traveled to an area near behind his right ear and McConnell drew in a sharp breath.

"You like that?" she said in a soft tone.

McConnell's face was reddening. "Yes."

Sam leaned down and whispered in his ear. "I'll make sure to give it extra special attention then."

Grabbing the bottle of Head and Shoulders, she went to work.

Chapter 9

Buster should have known there would be a bump in the road eventually. Cloning McConnell's phone and breaking into his house had both been a piece of cake. Now what were they going to do?

They hadn't even scratched the surface of McConnell's computer, but someone was in the house.

Max had quickly closed and re-locked the door, while Buster turned off the computer screen. How would they get the information they needed if whoever was in the house stuck around? Furthermore, how would they leave if they decided to chill in the kitchen?

"Oh, that's a marvelous idea, Fletcher!" McConnell's wife said in a playful tone.

Fletcher? Buster wrinkled his nose. He recognized Bettie's voice from her Live videos on her page, but the name Fletcher was unfamiliar. Her and McConnell hadn't mentioned anyone named Fletcher in their text messages to each other. Who was...

Moaning and kissing sounds interrupted Buster's thoughts.

So that's who Fletcher was.

McConnell was cheating on his wife with the women at the fetish club, and she was cheating on him with Fletcher.

"Damn," Max whispered, as if reading Buster's thoughts.

Buster shrugged. "Hopefully they take it to the bedroom."

Sure enough, no sooner than he said the words did Bettie say, "Come on!" in an excited voice, then footsteps could be heard going down the hall. A light flipped on outside of the office door before the bedroom door shut. McConnell's house was only one floor with mostly an open concept. The bedroom was down the hall to the left of his office, while the kitchen was down the hall and through the living room and den to the right.

Buster resumed action on McConnell's computer, but he couldn't help but to become distracted at Bettie's moans and screams.

"Sounds like Fletcher is tearing it up!" He chuckled.

Max looked like he was grossed out but nodded in agreement.

The headboard began banging against the wall, and Buster and Max could no longer contain themselves. They doubled over in laughter at the irony of the situation. McConnell was so worried about his wife finding out about his fetish, while here she was with a whole other man on the side.

Once the laughter subsided, Buster went back to work.

Although it was easy to get into McConnell's computer, finding any information on Brighton Miller was much easier said than done. Fifteen minutes into his search, Bettie and Fletcher's moaning died down.

Buster was sifting through his thirtieth folder when he finally found one titled B.M. That had to be it. It was hidden within multiple other folders, and if Buster weren't focused, he would have never found it.

Of course, this folder had several other folders within it, so Buster continued. The first folder told him that he was correct that the initials stood for Brighton Miller. There were some documents with his plans to run again for public office.

Buster exited that folder and went to another one.

Seventeen folders later, he was giving up hope. There was only one folder left, and it was titled *Charity*.

Within the Charity folder, there were thirty two subfolders.

"This guy…" Buster swiped his hand down his face.

Max was busy throwing a paper ball in the air and catching it repeatedly. "Still nothing?"

Buster shook his head, his spirits dampened.

Every folder had a name attached to it. Buster's eyes scanned the list, picking up various organizations he recognized. There was one folder that caught his attention. It was labeled *New*.

He clicked it. When he did, there were several other subfolders, but one was labeled *S&S*. His gut told him that was the one. He clicked it, and what he found made his jaw drop.

***

Buster and Max were taking entirely too long with other people inside the house. Why hadn't they left yet?

Various visions of standoffs and knife fights tumbled through Shatina's mind. She hoped they were okay.

Reaching for her phone that was in a holder affixed to her air vent, she intended to text them and ask for an update.

Before her fingers could swipe the screen, a group text from Tamika showed up. Shatina read the message.

Okay, Miss Tara is doing a bit much. Road trip?

Shatina's ears pounded. They wanted to do a road trip?

She already knew how that situation would turn out. She couldn't let them go to Shatara's school, not when Shatina was so close to potentially finding her sister and getting her away from Brighton safely. She had to think quickly.

How about we hold off on that? she texted. *I just heard from her the other day.*

Oh yeah? Tyonne texted. *Well, why is she answering you, but not us?*

Right! Tamika added. *I thought we agreed to work on our relationship, not let it go back to the way it was.*

Shatina couldn't think of a response for that one. She had to do something, and soon.

***

Sam had originally been weirded out by McConnell's fetish, but as she massaged his scalp and watched his reactions, she found herself having fun.

McConnell had grown extremely comfortable with their arrangement. Less than five minutes into the shampooing session, his belt was unbuckled and his hand was in his pants.

Sam focused her thoughts on Robert, imagining that she was causing him the level of pleasure she was bringing out of McConnell.

The man was in a state of pure ecstasy, writhing back and forth, begging her not to stop. When he pulled out his pulsing member, Sam's eyes widened for more reasons than one.

Who knew McConnell was packing like that?

"Okay, Miss Bettie!" she mouthed, and continued, allowing her fingers to massage the spot near his right ear that he liked so much.

Within seconds, McConnell's body jerked and he reached his release.

She stood behind him, wiping her hands with a towel before turning off her camera and placing the device back inside her bra.

McConnell's eyes were closed as his breathing returned to normal.

"Would you like me to rinse you?" Sam asked in a seductive tone.

"Hm?" he asked, sounding distracted at first. "Oh, no dear. I'm all set. I'll take it from here. You've been lovely, and those fingers are more magical than I suspected."

Sam giggled, pleased that he enjoyed her performance. "Sure you don't want another round?"

McConnell shook his head, then his smile wavered. "No, I'm afraid I have to get home to my wife."

"Wife?" she repeated as if she were surprised.

His cheeks tinged with embarrassment. "Yes, my wife." He spoke in a hollow tone. "She doesn't know about my... about what I like."

Sam gasped. "You never told her?"

A tear slid down his cheek, and Sam's heart panged for him.

"No, I'm afraid I haven't. She'll probably divorce me."

Sam tried to reassure him. "I'm sure she wouldn't. Why not broach the subject with her? She might like it just as much as you."

McConnell's demeanor stiffened. "She won't. My wife is the love of my life, but she would never go for something like this. She's very shy in the bedroom."

Sam decided to leave it there. "I understand." She nodded. "I guess I'll see you around?"

The corners of McConnell's lips turned up. "Sure. Actually, do you mind exchanging usernames?"

Sam smiled. "Sure. I'm SexyButterfly69."

"Ooh, spicy!"

Sam chuckled. "I'll see you around, Dirty Boy."

Chapter 10

Max, Shatina, Buster, and Sam had agreed to meet at the cabin after their various excursions to debrief each other on what they found.

Max, Shatina, and Buster rode together, while Sam was coming from the party at McConnell's club.

Shatina was frustrated, to say the least.

After spending over an hour inside McConnell's house, Max and Buster didn't want to tell her what they found.

"Why not?" she asked.

Max stared straight ahead. "It's best if we wait until everyone is together before we discuss it." The way he said it caused alarm bells to ring in Shatina's mind. What was the big secret? Three out of the four of them were in the car. Why couldn't they tell her what they found and fill Sam in later? Shatara was her sister, not Sam's.

Shatina didn't like the sound of this.

They couldn't get to the cabin soon enough. When they finally arrived, Sam was already there, pulling off her wig, slipping out of her stilettos and into some thick wool socks before putting on her knee-high boots.

"I hope you guys found something good, because this video isn't much," she said.

They watched as she popped out her contacts, then threw them in the trash.

"Can I see?" Buster said, looking intrigued as he reached for her cell phone on the table.

Sam shrugged. "Sure, but I must warn you, he gets a little graphic toward the end."

Buster's hand dropped back to his side. "Never mind."

"What did you two find?" Shatina pressed, staring back and forth between Max and Buster.

Buster shot Sam an uneasy look, then Max, before he suggested they all sit down.

***

Sam studied Max and Buster as they stared at each other, neither of them speaking.

"Well?" she gestured.

Their silence was making her nervous.

Buster spoke slowly. "We saved everything we found to the flash drive." He stared at Max, but Max said nothing, he just stared at Shatina.

"And?" Sam urged. They needed to come out with it already.

Buster and Max shared another glance. "It's bad," Buster said.

"Is she still alive?" Shatina asked.

Max nodded. "We think so."

"Did they reveal her location?" Sam asked.

Max swallowed. "No."

"What did you find, then?" Shatina urged.

Another uneasy glance. "It's not good."

"Okay, you already said that. What is it, Max? We don't have all night!"

Buster cut in. "Brighton's been dealing more than drugs."

Shatina paused. "Okay... what does that mean?"

Silence filled the room again.

The wheels were turning in Sam's mind, but Shatina appeared to be in denial.

Max spoke next, grabbing her hand. "Babe, Brighton was never planning to return Shatara to us."

Shatina's eyes clouded. "What do you mean?"

Max looked away, so Buster continued.

"He's having an auction in a week."

"An auction?"

Buster nodded.

"What for?"

Shatina knew what he was telling her, Sam could tell. She just wanted to hear it to erase all possible doubt.

Buster spelled it out. "Brighton's been involved in trafficking for at least three years. He's planning to ship Shatara out of the country."

Shatina's eyes bugged out. "Shipping her out of the country? Where is she?" She turned to Max. "Where is my sister, Max?"

A tear formed in the corner of Max's eyes. "We don't know, babe."

"How can you not know? McConnell didn't have the location stored in his office?"

Buster shook his head. "No, we looked everywhere Shatina. I swear."

Shatina shook her head in disbelief. "So you're telling me that my sister is going to be sold to some sick disgusting man for his own pleasure, and we have no way of getting to her to stop it."

No one answered.

Shatina was still for a moment, then she began to hyperventilate.

Max jumped into action, his eyes locking with Sam's. "Get her some water, please?" He held her as Sam wordlessly jumped up and ran to the refrigerator. She returned with the water bottle and placed it in front of Shatina, but Shatina lashed out and swiped it off the table. It flew across the room and hit the wall. She began rocking back and forth, her forehead creased with agony, while Max tried to reassure her.

"Babe, we'll get her back. I swear."

Chapter 11

Shatara was trying to cling to a sliver of hope, but it was dwindling fast. She had sent her location to Shatina but was moved that same night.

She wondered if Brighton had found out about the email? If he had, he never mentioned it. How was she going to get out of here?

This time when they moved her, they were more careful and she wasn't able to see anything. She knew she was in a basement because of the fact that she was carried down some stairs. Also, this building wasn't abandoned like the last one, because when the door at the end of the hall opened, she could hear faint sounds of activity from outside it. When the door shut, however, she heard nothing at all. The basement must have been soundproof.

Shatara shuddered to think of what that could possibly mean.

She had no more tears left to cry. She had to find a way out of this place since she had a funny feeling Brighton wasn't going to let her go, regardless of whether Shatina and Max turned themselves in.

Previously, she had hoped that her sister would come to find her, but how could she? Shatara didn't know what kind of resources her twin had available. What if she had given up and decided to let Shatara go? Would Shatina do such a thing?

That thought marinated a few moments. Shatara didn't want to think her sister would give up on her without a fight, but it was possible.

This wasn't some hostage movie; this was real life. And in real life, Shatina was no Liam Neeson. She was a young woman, barely out of her teens, who followed a voice in her head for advice.

That was harsh, and Shatara knew it, but she couldn't help but to feel bitter.

Her wrists and ankles were blistered, and her shoulders felt like they would never be the same again, not to mention the fact that her bottom had gone completely numb. She was stuck here, tied to a chair, and there wasn't a thing she could do about it.

Shatara sat in darkness for God knew how long before the door at the end of the hallway opened and she heard footsteps coming in her direction. Esmeralda, from the sound of it.

She was right. Esmeralda entered the room carrying Shatara's dinner on a tray, along with a drink.

Shatara still wasn't allowed to feed herself, so she prepared to endure another demeaning meal.

An indiscernible look shone in Esmeralda's eyes, but Shatara wasn't sure whether she should question it. Instead, she began the daily ritual of opening her mouth to receive spoonful's of chicken noodle soup.

Once she finished the soup, Esmeralda held the cup of lemonade to her lips. "I forgot the straw," she said in broken English. Her words almost caused Shatara to choke, for more reasons than one. This was the first time she'd ever heard the woman speak, and the look in her eyes when she said it was as if she was trying to communicate a message.

Esmeralda nodded at the cup, and Shatara's gaze trailed downward.

There was something in the bottom of the cup. Something rectangular and metal.

Shatara nodded, and Esmeralda continued to hold the cup to her lips until she finished. Once the lemonade was gone, Esmeralda tipped the cup one last time, allowing the razor blade to fall into Shatara's waiting mouth.

When Shatara received it, she nodded, and Esmeralda removed the cup, but now looked afraid.

Shatara nodded again to let her know she wouldn't tell on her.

Esmeralda's eyes clouded, then she turned and swiftly exited the room. Now Shatara just had to find a way to use the blade to cut the ropes.

***

It took the entire crew to calm Shatina, but Max knew it would only be a matter of time before she blew up again. The cabin was almost destroyed because of the flipped table and overturned chairs. Not to mention the broken glass. Shatina had lost it, and there was nothing anyone could do to fix it.

Brighton Miller was planning to sell her sister, and Shatara could be anywhere in the city. They had no way of finding her. Max didn't want to give up hope, but it was hard not to.

He drove Shatina home, and her sobs of anguish almost caused him to pull over and start crying himself. He knew he couldn't do that though. He had to be strong for his woman. Before they pulled up to Shatina's apartment, Max had an idea. Maybe he could turn himself in to the police in exchange for Shatara. He didn't think Brighton would give her back, but he had to exhaust all options. Maybe the man possessed a shred of integrity, somewhere within the evil fabric of his soul.

He thought to broach the idea with Shatina when they got inside. They exited the car and walked up to her front door. Shatina had her head down as she walked, so she didn't notice it, but Max saw an envelope taped to her front door. Without saying anything, Max snatched it.

Shatina heard it and looked up.

He gave her an uneasy glance.

"What is that?" she asked.

He shrugged. "I have no idea. There's nothing written on the outside."

Shatina's eyes filled with hope. "Open it."

Max stared at her, not sure if that was a good idea. They had already had a rough night. Shatina couldn't take anymore bad news.

"Let's go inside."

They entered the apartment and Shatina snatched the envelope from Max's hands before he had a chance to react.

"Don't!" he said, reaching for it, but she was already ripping it open.

A single sheet of paper was inside.

Max's heart palpitated as he watched Shatina scan the page.

She gasped in shock.

"Max, we got her!"

Max was confused. "What do you mean?"

"Look!" She held out the paper and pointed. "Shatara! Someone gave us the location."

Max stammered as he spoke. "Someone gave us the… how?" His mind was swimming with possibilities. Who could have possibly known what was going on and given them this information? This had to be a trap.

"Do you see the address?" Shatina asked, the excitement returning to her eyes. "She's at McConnell's club, in the basement. Sam was right above her the whole night and never knew it."

Shatina was acting delirious now, and Max was worried. They had to think clearly in this situation. "Shatina, I understand you're excited, but how do we know this is true? What if it's a trap."

"It's not! We're going there. Let's call Buster and Sam right now."

"Shatina…" Max started, but she was already pulling out her phone.

Buster and Sam arrived in less than an hour, and the crew spent the rest of the night developing a plan.

Max wasn't sure if it would work, or if they were leading themselves to their doom, but he hoped like hell for the former.

Who had sent the information though? That was the million-dollar question.

Chapter 12

Max and Jared bore virtually no resemblance to one another. Not that Shatina expected them to, since Max was adopted, but still. Max was tall, while Jared was Shatina's height. Jared displayed a tough exterior, while Max looked like a hot nerd. They were both good looking, just in different ways. Jared was light skinned, while Max had more of a caramel complexion. Jared bore three teardrop tattoos below one of his eyes, while not a trace of ink could be found on Max's body.

"Hey everyone, this is Jared," Max said, introducing his brother to the crew.

Jared nodded at Buster but gave Shatina and Max each a smile and a short wave.

Is he shy? Shatina was surprised. From the way Max described his brother, he was reckless and full of bravado. Shatina never would have guessed he was shy around women. *Or maybe* some *women*, she thought, because she remembered Max said Jared was throwing dollars at strippers not too long ago.

She refocused. No time for psychoanalysis. They needed to keep their attention on the matter at hand.

Shatina smiled back at Jared. "Thank you for agreeing to help us. I really appreciate it."

Jared blushed. "No doubt. Anything for the family."

Max spoke next. "Hey, do you think Rambo or any of your other guys would help us?"

Jared waited a beat before responding. "I could ask. I'm sure he wouldn't mind. I'll make some calls."

Now Jared's bravado was rising to the surface.

"Did Max tell you the plan?" Sam asked.

Jared shook his head. "He said you guys would explain when we met."

"Cool," Buster said. "Here's what we have so far."

The plan was going to be a lot easier to explain than to carry out. They had to sneak into McConnell's club, find their way to the basement where they hoped Shatara would still be, get her out, and make it home safely without being spotted.

The club would be full of people for another masquerade party. The parties were a cover for Brighton's true operation.

When Buster finished speaking, Jared stared at him intently. "Do you know how to handle a gun?"

Buster shook his head. "No, not really."

Jared was silent for a moment before he spoke his next words. "I'll call my guys."

When they left the cabin, Shatina felt like the plan was reinforced. She turned to Max, who was driving her home. "Do you really think we'll be able to pull this off?"

Max offered her a small smile. "We've accomplished all our missions so far."

That part was true, but this was the riskiest mission of them all, and they had much more to lose than Shatina could bear. If they didn't get her sister out of that building during the party, she might never see her again.

Chapter 13

Now that Jared was on board, Max considered enlisting Ted. He wasn't sure about that idea though, since he'd literally just met the man, and the fact that he had avoided his last few calls and texts.

Life was too complicated right now for a family reunion.

As if reading his thoughts, Ted's number displayed on the dashboard. Max glanced at Shatina, then pressed the button to answer it.

"Hey."

"Hey, Max. Long time no see."

"I know."

Ted was silent for a moment before he spoke again. "You driving?"

"Yeah."

"Where are you headed?"

"Dropping Shatina off."

"Oh…" Ted chuckled. "Hot date?"

Max forced himself to relax. How was he ever going to build a relationship with his father if he gave him one-word answers? He may have come way too late to play a role in Max's growing up years, but at least Ted was trying now.

"No, we had a meeting. What have you been up to?"

Ted's tone lightened considerably. "Nothing much. Just torturing a new class of students. Ask Shatina about it. She knows."

Max caught a glance at Shatina rolling her eyes.

"How's your new semester going, Shatina?"

"Just fine, Ted." She sighed.

"What's up with y'all? Did you two just have an argument or something? Why do you sound so tense?"

"We're not tense," they answered in unison.

Ted was silent for a few more moments. "Well, I won't hold you Max. I just wanted to see how you're doing. Feel free to call me sometime too."

Max didn't miss the disappointment in Ted's tone.

He understood where the man was coming from, but Ted had to know that meeting his biological father after all these years had come out of nowhere. By the time Max graduated high school, he had written off his biological parents forever. If they hadn't tried to reach out to him by that point, why would they when he was an adult?

"I gotchu," Max answered, and they ended the call.

They pulled up to Shatina's apartment.

"Do you think you two will build a bond after everything is over?" Shatina asked.

Max shrugged. "I hope so, but at the same time, it feels weird. To go from having parents who wanted me at first, then discarded me when Jared came... To holding out hope for my biological parents to come back for me then giving up. And now I find out my mother is dead and my father's a college professor. It's too much to process right now."

Shatina nodded. "I understand."

She reached out and grabbed his hand. No words were needed. He understood that she was telling him that just like he would be there for her, she would be there for him through his troubles too.

Chapter 14

It was ironic that as soon as Max and Shatina entered Shatina's apartment after Max's conversation with Ted, Shatina received a phone call from her mother.

Shatina's breath caught in her throat. She already knew what this was about. What could she possibly say?

She moved to answer it but chickened out at the last second.

"Who is that?" Max asked.

"My mother." Shatina's hands started shaking.

Her mother called again.

Shatina swallowed. "I don't know what to say."

Max looked like he was thinking, but he couldn't come up with anything either. Shatina answered before the ring ran out a second time.

"Hello?"

Her mother launched right into it. "Shatina, where is your sister?" Her voice boomed into the phone like she meant business.

Shatina gulped. "What do you mean, where is she?"

"Don't play with me. This is not time for games. I have been calling Shatara for over a week, but I figured she was still mad at me about our disagreement, so I was giving her time to cool off. I tried to call her again today, but she's still not answering."

Shatina's mind was reeling. She had almost forgotten about the argument between Shatara and their mother before they left for school from Winter Break. Shatara had asked their parents to take out another loan so she could study abroad, and their mother said no. The dark irony of Shatara's current situation struck Shatina at that moment, but she refused to dwell on it.

"I'll try to call her," Shatina offered.

"No, I don't want you to call her. I want you to tell me where she is."

Shatina struggled to understand exactly what her mother was saying, and how much she might have known.

"What do you mean, where is she?"

Her mother sighed. "Shatina, I know she's not at school. You wouldn't believe the drama I had to go through to get some answers, but she took a leave of absence at the beginning of the semester."

Shatina gasped. "A leave of absence?"

"Yes. The school wouldn't even tell me that. I was worried, so I called. They gave me the runaround before finally telling me that it was against the law for them to reveal confidential information, despite the fact that I was her parent. I had to look up her roommate on the internet and beg her to help me. She asked Shatara's RA, who was doing an internship at the Registrar's office. The RA told Shatara's roommate about the leave of absence, and the roommate told me."

"Wow."

"I'll ask you again, Shatina, where is your sister? This is not like her to dodge calls for so long, and then just up and disappear. Is she pregnant? Why won't she talk to me?"

Shatina swallowed as her mind flashed to Tyonne, who still hadn't told her parents about her pregnancy. "No, I don't think she's pregnant. I'll reach out to her."

"Do you know where she is?"

It was as if Shatina were in an interrogation room, and her mother was playing bad cop. Shatina wanted to come clean and tell her what happened, but she knew that would only make a bad situation worse.

Still, if she didn't tell and they weren't able to help Shatara escape, her sister would be gone forever and it would be all Shatina's fault.

"Hello?" Her mother was growing impatient.

Shatina snapped out of it. "I'm sorry. No, Mom, I don't know where she is. I'll call her and if she answers, I'll tell her to call you."

"Bye, Shatina!" Her mother hung up in her face.

She hated the fact that she had to lie, but what made matters worse was that her mother didn't believe her, and if things didn't go according to plan, she would probably disown her forever.

Chapter 15

Sam was on her third date with Brighton, but she was growing increasingly disgusted with him as time wore on. What could she have possibly seen in such a man? Sex trafficking young women for the past three years?

How the hell had she missed that?

If she hadn't been so busy plotting and scheming against other people, maybe she would have picked up on it.

Now she had to sit and smile in this man's face, knowing that the devil resided within him. Not to mention that her relationship with Ted was on thin ice as it was. With the weight of what was going on with Shatina's sister over her head, Sam was stressed beyond belief. She wanted this situation to be over so she could move on with her life.

Sooner or later, if she didn't change, Ted would leave her.

"Wanna come to my place for a nightcap?" Brighton flashed her his signature smile at the end of the evening.

This was his third request in a row. Sam couldn't say no this time, or he would start to suspect her. They had never gone this long without having sex before.

Still, if she could put it off any longer, she would take the opportunity. "Brighton, it's too soon."

Disappointment filled his eyes. "What do you mean, it's still too soon? Sam, is there someone else? You've been acting weird lately."

"What do you mean, acting weird?"

"I know you're upset with me, but you've never held out this long. You know you miss Zaddy." His devilish smirk was back.

Sam internally recoiled at his words but forced a seductive smile of her own. "I admit that I do, but you still need to pay for your disloyalty."

He gave her a puppy dog look. "Baby, I promise I won't stray again. It was only that one time, and technically, we were on a break."

"The break was because you lied to me. And while you were supposed to be thinking about that, you ended up with another woman."

Brighton sighed. "I know, and I'm sorry. Truly, I am. But can a guy catch a break for just one night? It's been way too long and these cold showers are no longer cutting it."

Sam thought about it. If she went to his house, maybe she could wait til he fell asleep to do some creeping. Perhaps there was more valuable intel that could be learned that would help their plan. Maybe she could even get him talking about the party.

"Okay." She reluctantly agreed. "But just this once, then you're back in the doghouse until I'm good and ready."

Brighton's face lit up. "I promise I'll be on my best behavior."

***

Shatina and Max were awakened by a knock on the front door. Both of their heads popped up, tension creased across their foreheads.

"Who is that?" Max asked. Shatina shrugged, then walked over.

"No, let me," Max whispered, but she was already calling out.

"Who is it?"

"Me!" Shatina's mother said.

Max and Shatina shared a fearful look. This was bad. Thankfully, Max's car wasn't parked directly in front of her door, so Shatina's mother wouldn't notice it, but what if she wanted to inspect the house and search for Shatara? Max couldn't be here.

"I'll go out back," he whispered, and Shatina nodded.

"Hold on, Mom!" she called out, as Max scrambled to straighten out the living room and fold the comforter they had laid under while they slept. Shatina watched as he stuffed the comforter into the hallway closet, then slipped on his coat and shoes before exiting the back door.

***

Shatina opened the front door and got the shock of her life. Not only was her mother outside, but she was standing next to a cop!

Shatina's heart dropped. This was it. The plan was over and her and Max were going to jail. How could she possibly pull this off?

"Mom, what is this?" Shatina asked, forcing the nervousness out of her tone.

Her mother studied her, hand on hip. "I knew you weren't telling me the truth over the phone. I explained to the officer that your sister was missing, and he agreed to help me follow up with you."

Shatina couldn't believe her ears. Her mother sold her out to the police? Why would she do such a thing? Then she shook the thought from her mind. Her mother wasn't selling her out. She was worried about her other daughter. Any mother would do what it took to get to the bottom of her child's disappearance if she suspected something was wrong. Shatina had to play this safe.

The officer chuckled as if he was trying to break the tension. "Let's calm for a second, ladies. Remember, we're not here to question your daughter. We're just checking in like we discussed." He focused on Shatina's mother as he spoke, and his tone of voice and body language let Shatina know that he thought her mother was overreacting.

Thank God, she thought, and decided to play that to her advantage.

Almost an hour later, Shatina's mother stormed out of her house, furious, while the officer looked nonchalant. Shatina slid down the wall to the floor, completely devoid of energy.

The lies were piling up, day by day. This situation was stretching her beyond belief. She had just betrayed her mother, in addition to creating more legal issues for herself if the truth ever came out.

Then there was the fact that if they weren't able to save Shatara... A tear slid down her cheek and she didn't bother to wipe it away.

She heard the back door open as Max reentered the apartment. "What happened?" he asked, but she couldn't form the words to answer him.

Chapter 16

Shatara had been holding the razor blade in her mouth for what felt like hours. Someone usually came to untie her after dinner so she could use the bathroom before bedtime, but tonight they were running late.

She had almost cut her tongue multiple times, moving the blade around to swallow excess saliva. Her mind didn't want to entertain the thought of where the blade had come from or what type of germs could have been on it before she took it from Esmeralda.

Shatara thought of her mother. Had she grown suspicious by now as to her whereabouts? Surely, someone outside of Shatina had to have noticed she was missing by now. Why hadn't anyone called the police? Or if they had, why hadn't Brighton mentioned it? Was that why he moved her from the abandoned building? To throw them off his scent?

Her thoughts were interrupted by Ate's footsteps. Shatara had memorized all their sounds by now. Ate's footsteps were the heaviest, while Brighton and Tony's were more lightweight, and Esmeralda's steps could barely be heard.

"Ready for a bathroom break?" he asked with a smile.

Shatara nodded without speaking. She sat still as Ate untied her hands first, then her feet. Her mind flashed with the thought of running for the door, but she knew she would never make it. Despite his hefty size, she was sure Ate could outrun her. She couldn't risk it. It was better to stick to her original plan of transferring the razor blade from her mouth to her hands in the bathroom, then cutting the rope when he left. She was usually alone for hours after the final bathroom break of the day.

Ate walked with her to the bathroom door, then watched as she cracked it to relieve herself. He whistled outside the door as she washed her hands. She carefully slid the blade between her left index and middle fingers, praying he wouldn't notice it when he tied her hands back up.

When she emerged from the bathroom, he continued to whistle as he walked her back to her seat. Another thought of running top speed toward the door flashed through her mind, but she knew she couldn't chance it. She felt like the dog she read about in her introductory psychology class. *Learned helplessness.* The dog had been chained up for so long that even when the owner unchained him, he still didn't try to leave the yard.

Anger coursed through her body at that thought. Where had her fight gone? She was leaving this building tonight.

Ate re-tied her ankles first, then moved to the back of the chair to grab her wrists. "Damn, Ma. Your wrists are starting to blister. We have to get you some Vaseline or something."

Starting to blister? It had been several days since the blisters began, but Shatara refused to answer him. Her mind was on freedom.

Ate finally left, and as soon as he exited the room, Shatara sprang into action. It would probably take a while to cut through the thick ropes with such a tiny blade, but it was certainly sharp enough to do the trick. Shatara began the process of slicing across the same spot repeatedly, then pulling as hard as she could. At first, it didn't seem like the blade was making any progress and sweat trickled down her back from all her efforts, but she continued.

Finally, the rope started to give.

Filled with renewed vigor, Shatara sliced faster. Finally, she tugged and felt a satisfying snap. Her hands were free. She bent forward to work on her ankles. They were much quicker to release.

She stood and felt dizzy with giddiness, unable to believe that she had broken herself free from the ropes. Now it was the moment of truth. About a hundred or so steps to the door that led to the stairwell, then it was only up from there.

Shatara breathed a quick prayer before creeping across the floor. She hoped no one was in the hallway. She approached the door but was afraid to open it.

Taking a deep breath, she inched it open and poked her head out, staring down the hall in both directions. No one was there. She softly closed the door behind her and crept toward the hallway door. Her heart was pounding the entire way.

Halfway to her destination, she heard a door at the other end of the hall open, then shut.

She didn't bother to look back as she ran the rest of the way toward the hallway door, hearing Ate hurl a few expletives as he raced behind her.

She made it to the door and pushed it open with all her might, but she overestimated how heavy it was and lost her balance.

Her elbow cracked against the cement floor, but she flipped over to stand, rushing up the stairs. She only got halfway up before she was yanked backward by Ate's strong arms. She screamed and wrestled against him, but it was no use. He was ten times stronger than her, and she had lost the blade when she fell.

"Let me go!" she screamed, trying to connect her foot with his groin.

"Shut up!" He grunted, clamping a hand over her mouth as he forced her back through the door and pushed her roughly down the hall.

Shatara struggled with all her might, but her efforts were in vain. When they got back into the room, Ate threw her to the floor. Shatara turned around and backed away from him as he inched toward her.

"You're lucky I can't put my hands on you." He sneered. "If I could, that pretty face of yours would be rearranged."

Shatara couldn't take the coldness in his eyes.

"Why don't you just let me go?" she cried. "I haven't done anything to anyone."

Ate opened his mouth to answer, but before he could, Brighton Miller opened the door and strode into the room.

"What the hell is going on here?"

Chapter 17

Sam's guilt was pushing her toward a nervous breakdown. She slept with Brighton after their last date, and not only did he not give her any information she could use to help the plan, but the sex wasn't even good. She had to pretend Brighton was Robert, because despite his usual stellar performance, her heart wasn't in it.

Now she was disgusted with herself.

As she had the thought, Buster texted her phone. *Dirty Boy wants you. Sixteen messages and counting. Should I answer?*

Sam had almost forgotten about the sex party app. Looked like McConnell wanted more of her *magical fingers,* as he called them. She shook her head and didn't bother to respond, returning her phone to her pocket.

"What are you thinking about?" Robert asked.

They were sitting in cushioned lawn chairs on his back deck, sipping hot cocoa and looking at the stars. If Sam wasn't so preoccupied with dark thoughts she would have embraced the romantic vibes Robert was giving off.

Sam shrugged. "Nothing. This is nice."

Robert cracked a grin. "You like my style, huh?"

Sam smiled back. "Indeed I do."

He stared at her, the intensity between them building before he leaned over and pressed his lips against hers.

She complied and allowed herself to sink into the kiss.

This was what she needed - who she needed. Robert. With him, she didn't have to focus on troubles or worries. With Robert, there was no guilt. She was free.

"I love you," he murmured, his voice so low that Sam barely heard him. It took her a few moments to register what he said, but when she realized that she hadn't been hearing things, she responded in kind.

"I love you too."

Before that moment, Sam hadn't recognized that love was what she was feeling. She had liked men before, cared for men before, but she could never say she had been in love. Until now.

Sitting back in her chair after the kiss, Sam decided to take the remainder of the evening and focus on what mattered. Yes, the plan was still lingering over their heads, but she didn't have to think about it every waking moment of the day.

When the plan was over, Robert would still be here. She couldn't keep disappointing him by closing herself off. It was time to let him in.

"I wish nights like this could last forever," she mused.

Robert squeezed her fingers gently. "Me too."

Sam took a final sip of cocoa, then sniffed, pressing her upper lip against the tip of her nose to warm it. Despite the skies being clear, it was still quite chilly.

"Want to go in and let me warm you up?" Robert asked in a suggestive tone.

Sam blushed and nodded, then an image of Brighton flashed in her mind. She shook it off, refusing to let her mind stay there.

Robert stood, and she followed suit.

"After you," he gestured, and Sam led the way inside.

Chapter 18

Shatina had no idea why she was still trying to submit assignments with everything that was going on, but she was. Maybe it was a coping mechanism or a way to maintain a shred of sanity as the day of the party approached. She finished a long day of classes and wanted nothing more than to go home and relax.

When she arrived, the house smelled like spaghetti. There were candles lit throughout the living room leading to the kitchen.

Shatina walked into the kitchen and saw Max, who was playing slow songs on her Bluetooth speaker while stirring meat and sauce in a pan.

She couldn't help but blush at his efforts. "What's all this?" She gestured.

He turned to face her and grinned. "I wanted to do something nice for you to take your mind off things."

Shatina's eyes watered. Max was giving her a gift that she didn't know she needed.

"Thank you."

"No problem."

Shatina sat at the table as Max fixed their plates, then they dug in. Just like last time, Max's spaghetti was slamming.

She watched Max eat for a few moments, feeling her temperature rise. When he finished his plate, she was about to say something, but he abruptly stood.

"Where are you going?" she asked, watching him walk toward the living room.

He smirked. "I'll be right back."

Shatina finished her meal, then put both of their dishes in the sink. She busied herself by washing them while she waited for Max to return.

When he did, he had a big smile on his face, but there was no indication of where he had just gone.

"What?" Shatina asked.

Max held out his hand for her to come to him. "Follow me."

She felt awkward, but giddy as she followed Max to her bathroom, where he had more candles set up, along with a bubble bath.

"Wow, this is beautiful." She turned to him. "Thank you, Max."

"Anything to see you smile."

Max left the bathroom and Shatina slid into the sudsy water, immediately feeling her body relax. The scent of lavender wafted into her nostrils. Her eyes rolled back. Max had no idea what he had just done.

Sometime later, Shatina emerged, her skin soft and slightly wrinkled.

It was at that moment she realized she didn't bring a change of clothes with her. *Oops.* A naughty idea flashed through her mind. Max had held out long enough. It was time to see what he was working with.

Shatina wrapped herself in a towel and exited the bathroom, throwing her dirty clothes in a hamper in the closet next to her bathroom on her way to the bedroom. Max was in her room holding a bottle of oil. He had really thought of everything.

"What's that?" She pointed at the bottle.

Max stared at her. "I wanted to make you feel good."

Shatina smirked and sauntered over to him. When he saw the seductive look in her eyes, he swallowed, his Adam's apple bobbing up and down.

That let Shatina know he was down for her to flip the script.

"How about I make you feel good instead?" she asked, then took the bottle from him and began pulling at his shirt.

Max immediately caught her drift and pulled off his own shirt and wife beater, revealing his neatly toned abs.

The intensity of the moment began to hit Shatina. They were really doing this, after all the time they'd known each other. Who would have thought she would be so taken by Max?

Max didn't give her much time to process that train of thought, because he regained control of the moment with a passionate kiss.

Shatina wrapped her arms around his neck and raised her thigh, motioning for him to lift her. He complied, then backed her against the wall.

She began fumbling with the zipper of his jeans, her body heated beyond belief. That bath had done something to her. He held her bottom against his waist as she slid his pants and boxers down.

Now they were both breathing heavily.

Shatina grew afraid. What if things didn't work out between them? What if her and Max weren't a good match after all? What if...?

Max positioned his hardened member against her core, licking and sucking on her neck while he simultaneously rubbed himself up and down her slit.

"Shhh...." Shatina swore. Just that quickly, all her doubtful thoughts were erased. She angled her legs wider to receive him.

He teased her a few moments longer before gently but forcefully sliding in.

Shatina gasped. It had been a while, and Max was bigger than Seth. From the way he was stroking, he was better too. She had half a mind to tell him to stop. She wasn't ready for this. When he pulled back slightly and bit his bottom lip before rounding his hips at another angle, she changed her mind.

They found a perfect rhythm, their bodies moving in sync.

Shatina could feel him heating up inside of her.

His eyes rolled back. "Shatina..." His voice wavered as he began thrusting harder. His facial expression grew more aggressive as he neared his climax.

A wave grew from the pit of Shatina's stomach and traveled through her body as she jerked in a release of her own. Her mouth formed an involuntary *O* and she screamed as Max's knees buckled.

He almost dropped her but caught himself as he let her legs down so she was in a standing position.

They stared into each other's eyes as they regained control of their labored breathing.

"That was..." Shatina started, but Max cut her off with another kiss.

Chapter 19

Sam and Robert were lying in bed together after making love for the third time in a row. Robert stroked her hair while she caressed his other arm.

"Did I help you take your mind off your troubles?" he asked in a low tone.

Sam chuckled. "You sure did." She leaned up to kiss him.

Before their embrace could deepen, Robert's phone began buzzing on his nightstand.

"Who is that?" Sam asked.

"Nobody more important than you." Robert repositioned himself so that he was on top of her again.

Sam stared into his eyes with surprise. "You're ready for another round?"

He smirked. "I am if you are."

His phone began buzzing again.

"Ugh, that's so annoying. Can you tell them to call back or turn it off?"

"I gotchu." Robert leaned over to grab the phone and glanced at it, wrinkling his nose. "It's an unknown number. Looks like they texted me too."

Sam scrunched her face. "Why would they text you?"

Robert swiped his screen to check the message. When his body stiffened, Sam should have seen that as a bad sign, but she didn't catch it.

He tapped the screen and sounds of a man and woman moaning and groaning filled the room. Within seconds, Robert was off her and on his feet. There was a menacing look in his eyes. "Sam, what the hell is this?"

Sam knew what it was without watching the video. Brighton had done this.

"Robert, I can explain…"

"This is time-stamped from two days ago. Seriously?" Hurt and anger were etched across his features.

Sam's lower lip trembled. "Robert… I…"

"You what, Sam? What could you possibly tell me? There's no explanation except that you're cheating."

Sam snapped out of it. "I'm not, though! I…" Her voice trailed off.

Robert stepped further away from her as if she were a venomous snake. "When I asked you what was up with you, I thought you were still hurt about the situation with your father. I was trying to be there for you, but the whole time, he wasn't the one who was on your mind."

"It's not what you think."

"Get out of my bed, Sam."

His tone was so cold it broke her heart. Sam knew that nothing she could say to him would change his mind. As quickly as it started, her relationship with Robert was over.

She sniffled as she slid her panties on, then re-hooked her bra and stepped into her jeans. Robert stared at her as if he was contemplating throwing her out before she had a chance to finish putting her clothes back on.

She didn't know what to do.

Sam knew she should say something, do something, but she'd never been in a situation like this before. Not from the cheater's end.

She began walking toward his front door to grab her coat from the rack as Robert followed. The change in location from his bedroom to the den caused her to snap out of her trance.

She whirled around to face him. "Robert, please. You have to let me explain." She would tell him everything if it meant he would forgive her. Max and Shatina would be upset, but they didn't understand what she and Robert shared.

Robert stared straight ahead with dull eyes. "No need. I'm already past you, Ma."

His tone had such a bite to it, Sam felt like she had been slapped in the face. He couldn't mean that right? No way could he tell her he loved her, then treat her like she no longer existed.

When Robert slammed the door in her face right after she exited his house, Sam wasn't so sure of her assertions.

Chapter 20

Tonight was the night. Jared caught hold of a limo they all traveled in. Everyone changed their appearance slightly, from wigs to dyed hair to a change in style, and they all sported fake ID's along with their masks.

Shatina hoped their efforts were enough to make them unrecognizable.

Appearances aside, the toughest part of the evening would be sneaking in the back door. Buster was the only one besides Jared who the crew figured could get in the front door. Since there was a possibility that Brighton would know who Jared was because of his relation to Max, they didn't want to take any chances.

They watched as Buster approached the doorman with his fake ID. Shatina held her breath until he had safely entered.

Now they needed to drive around to the back to be let in, grab Shatara, and hopefully be out of the building before anyone noticed she was gone.

Jared was supposed to watch the back door while Buster led the group down to the basement to get Shatara.

Shatina looked at Sam, who was seated across from her. Sam was seated next to Rambo, Jared's friend, who had been eyeing her ever since he arrived. Sam looked so depressed that it almost caused Shatina to lose focus. She would have to talk to her later to ask what was going on.

Despite their prior drama and the current mess they were in, Sam had been nothing but solid on this mission. Shatina hoped that whatever she was going through behind the scenes was something that could be resolved.

Max grabbed Shatina's hand to get her attention. She faced him. He was seated next to her, while Jared was on his other side.

One of Jared's other guys, Slim, was driving.

Max's face held a solemn expression. "When we go in there, stay behind me, okay?"

Shatina nodded.

He turned to Sam. "You too, Sam."

A tear slid down her cheek, but Sam wiped it and nodded too.

Alarm bells rang in Shatina's mind. What was going on with Sam? She didn't know the girl that well, but it seemed that her personality had changed dramatically since the incident happened. She was very emotional lately.

Slim pulled around to the back of the building and the crew waited anxiously for Buster to open the back door.

Ten minutes later, he did, signaling that the coast was clear.

The crew filed out of the limo, sliding past Buster as they each entered the dimly lit hallway.

Music was blasting through the walls. Buster nodded toward another door. "Stairwell is that way."

Max led the way as he, Shatina, and Sam crept down the stairs. Buster was standing at the door to the stairwell, watching the halls for any activity.

Chapter 21

Shatara was cuffed to the chair this time, wearing a revealing red dress, eight-inch stilettos, and a face beat to perfection.

Brighton informed her that she would be leaving the country tonight. Shatara asked him, *"What do you mean, I'm leaving the country?"* But he didn't respond. Instead, he offered a sinister smile before backing out of the room.

Esmeralda had done her makeup. The bruise under her left eye was an indication that Ate must have told Brighton that she somehow tried to help her escape.

Shatara asked Esmeralda what Brighton meant when he said she was leaving the country, but Esmeralda didn't answer either. Her face was devoid of emotion as she applied a full face of makeup, including lashes to Shatara's features.

When Esmeralda exited the room, Shatara was left with nothing but her thoughts. Thoughts of how she got where she was, if she would ever find a way to escape, and what kind of evil plans Brighton had for her in another country.

Then it dawned on her.

His sinister smile.

The eerie way he spoke.

He wasn't...

Was he?

Shatara's heart dropped as she began struggling against the cuffs. She wrestled against the arms of the chair with all her might, trying desperately to break free. They wouldn't budge, so she screamed until her voice grew hoarse.

Vomit rose from the pit of her stomach and spurted out onto her dress. She couldn't go out like this. No way was something like that about to be her life.

Ate returned to the room and saw that she had thrown up down the front of her dress.

"You little..." he growled, hurling an expletive in her direction.

He stalked over and yanked her head back by her freshly pressed mane, then grabbed her throat and squeezed.

"I should kill you right now," he whispered. "Esmeralda!" he barked. "Come clean this up!"

Esmeralda rushed into the room, fear shining in her eyes.

Ate released Shatara's head. A migraine was beginning to form.

"You can't do this to me!" she screeched.

Ate's menacing expression changed to a grin. "Of course we can. You're already bought and sold, sweet thang."

Shatara cried as Esmeralda exited the room, then returned with another red dress. As if they had made provisions for this sort of thing.

Ate returned with his boy Tony and they all watched as Shatara changed into the new dress, then Esmeralda fixed her hair and makeup.

When she finished, they exited the room. Esmeralda shot her one last look of empathy before disappearing to the other side of the door.

Chapter 22

Max, Shatina, and Sam entered the basement. The hallway was dimly lit and lined with rooms on both sides. They would have to move quickly to find the door Shatara was housed behind and avoid stumbling upon any of Brighton's guys.

They quickly discovered that each room held a beautiful young woman who was dressed for the ages but tied or cuffed to a chair.

Max's heart sank to the pit of his stomach. He wished they could save them all but knew they couldn't.

Finally, they found her.

"Shatara!" Shatina whispered loudly.

Shatara looked up from her seated position, her eyes widened in shock. "What are you...? How are you...?"

Shatina wasted no time rushing over to embrace her sister, while Sam bent behind her to work on the cuffs that were binding her wrists to the back of the chair.

Max worked on her ankles. He had a much tougher time jimmying the locks than Sam did. Sam got Shatara's hands free in seconds, while Max was still struggling.

"Move," she whispered, and lay down on the floor to do it herself.

They used a different type of cuff for Shatara's ankles, so Sam had difficulty picking the lock. "Come on!" she whimpered, pounding the ground in frustration, then refocusing on the lock. Max stood with his eyes trained on the door, feeling out of place, while Shatina and Shatara stared at each other.

"How did you find me?" Shatara asked. The stained tears on her cheeks showed that she had been crying, and the blisters on her wrists betrayed some of the trauma she endured.

Shatina shook her head. "It's a long story. We'll tell you later, but first, we have to get you out of here."

"These damn things won't budge!" Sam said, exasperated, and Shatina bent to take over.

Sam sat on her bottom with her knees pulled up, staring straight ahead with a sullen expression.

"It's fine, we'll get her out," Max said in a reassuring tone. "You were able to free her wrists."

They heard a click as Shatina got one ankle free, but the other proved to be a serious problem. Shatara stood and used one of her heels to bang it against the rung of the wooden chair. She had almost cracked it when the door opened and another woman entered the room.

All of their heads whipped toward her in shock. No one had heard her coming.

The woman's eyes widened just as Shatara cracked the rung of the chair her ankle was cuffed to, then kicked herself free. She still had one half of the cuff around her ankle, but she was free.

"You have to move quickly!" the woman said, her body trembling with fear.

Before anyone could take a step, the door banged open, knocking the woman out of the way and a hulky, menacing man entered the room.

"What the hell is this?" he said, his eyes assessing the situation. Max rushed him, ready to fight, and the man was caught off guard so he bumped up against the wall. The two proceeded to scuffle, tussling toward the middle of the room.

Gunshots sounded from down the hall. There was no time for a fight. They had to get out. Max backed away and pulled out his gun, but before he could shoot, the other woman came from the side and plunged the heel of one of Shatara's stilettos into the bigger man's neck. They all watched as he toppled to the ground, blood gushing from where she stabbed him.

"Let's go!" Sam shouted, and they darted from the room.

There was no way out of the building but through the direction the shots were coming. Max swallowed and held his gun steady, leading the way.

Chapter 23

When they got to the stairwell, Buster and Jared were on the other side, coming their way. "We gotta go!" Buster shouted. "We just took out six guys!"

The crew bounded up the steps and into the hallway of the club, just as more men were coming from the other direction. They raised their guns, but Buster, Max, and Jared started shooting before they could make a move.

The women ran from the club and toward the limo while chaos ensued inside the building. Rambo was standing guard with a gun of his own, ready for action. He ran toward the building when he saw the women had made it outside safely.

The women tumbled inside the limo, scared out of their minds. They had no idea what was going on inside that building, but they knew it wasn't good.

Shatina was worried about all the men, but her mind was trained on Max. This couldn't be the end for him. They had gone through too much together.

Max was in there risking his life for her and her sister. He had to make it out alive.

"Who are you?" Sam asked the mysterious woman who had stabbed the man in Shatara's room.

The woman didn't answer. She shook her head as if to say, *please don't make me go back in there.*

"We're not going to hurt you," Shatina reassured her.

"Her name is Esmeralda," Shatara answered. "She's been helping me."

"Did they hurt you?" Shatina asked, but Shatara shook her head. "I don't want to talk about it right now. I just want to get the hell out of here."

As if they heard her words, all four guys came tumbling out of the back door of the club. Jared was in the lead, while Rambo held the rear.

They rushed toward the car, but more guys came around the corner from the front of the club, weapons drawn.

Chills ran down Shatina's spine at the sight of the standoff.

"We can do this the easy way, or the hard way," one of them said. "Give us back the girl, and we'll let you go in peace."

"That's not happening," Jared said.

"Then you leave us no choice."

Shatina braced herself as more shots rang out, but miraculously, only Brighton's men were falling due to being shot from behind. *What the hell?*

Everyone was confused as a figure emerged from the shadows.

"Who the hell is…?" Jared said, his gun pointing at the mysterious figure, while Shatina yelled, "Seth?"

Chapter 24

Indeed it was Seth, dressed in army fatigues and a black bulletproof vest.

"We totally should have thought of that," Jared said, when he noticed the vest.

Seth cracked a smile. "Glad to be of assistance."

Max gave him an awkward glance.

Shatina climbed out of the limo to face him. "Seth, what are you doing here?"

Seth stared at Shatina. "I came back for you."

Shatina was confused. "But why? How?"

Seth launched into the story. "You were right about Brighton no longer going to trial."

"Yes... and?" She persisted.

He sighed. "They told me I was no longer needed. The more I sat there, the more worthless I felt. I lost my parents, I lost my friends, but worst of all, I lost you. I knew it was way too much for me to ask you to go into protection with me. I was selfish and I'm sorry. Especially since I'm the one who got you in this whole situation anyway."

Shatina wasn't following. "How do you think you got me in this situation? What exactly do you know about what's been going on?"

Seth looked over his shoulder, and the rest of them did as well. No one was there, but Shatina knew they needed to leave soon before the police were called.

Seth continued. "I left town and came back here for you once they told me I was no longer needed. When I got here, I ran across my boy Tony, who runs with Brighton's crew. It turned out that Brighton played him out of a promotion, so Tony was willing to spill some details. He knew about our relationship, and he shared with me how Brighton had your sister. He showed me a picture and everything. I couldn't let him do that to her, Shatina. So I sent you the info, and prepared to be here myself tonight to make sure you got away safely."

"But how did you know I would come, and why not just say something to me?" Shatina was still confused.

Seth's face fell. "Tony told me about you and Max too. I remembered you said his name when we were together, and from that I reasoned that you two must be seeing each other."

Shatina swallowed. "But you came anyway."

Seth raised his head to face her and nodded.

"This is a great reunion and all, guys, but we gotta go," Jared said. As he spoke, the sounds of screeching tires came from multiple directions, along with the sounds of sirens in the distance.

They started diving into the limo, but not before more shots rang out.

Buster went down first, then Seth.

"No!" Shatina screamed.

Chapter 25

The next few moments happened so fast, Max's head was spinning. One second, they were standing around listening to Seth's story, and the next, chaos ensued, a half a dozen black vans pulled up, and Buster and Seth were lying in pools of blood.

It didn't take a rocket scientist to see that Seth was dead. Half his head was missing.

Buster was still moving though. He suffered a shot to the chest.

"Let's go," Jared yelled, ducking shots and shooting back as he, Max, and Rambo pulled Buster into the limo, then Slim peeled off before they had a chance to close the doors.

As they were turning the corner, Max saw the back door of the club open and girls being ushered into the black vans.

"Oh my God..." Sam said, grimacing at the sight of Buster, and worked with Shatara to apply pressure to his chest. More shots rang out behind them, and Max looked up to see a vehicle on their tail. Jared and Rambo were already on it, sliding down the windows and opening fire on whoever was behind them.

"You gotta go faster, Slim!" Rambo shouted.

"You realize this is a freaking limo, right?" Slim yelled back.

"We need to get him to a hospital!" Shatara said.

More gunshots sounded, and Max, Shatina, Shatara, and Sam put their heads down.

The limo started leaning to one side. "Shoot! We lost a tire!"

Max began to panic internally. *We're not going to make it out of this alive.*

No sooner than he had the thought, the limo ran through a lane of traffic, narrowly missing several vehicles, then the car behind them did too, but was bowled over by a tractor trailer.

Things were tense for a few moments as Slim pulled the limo into a junkyard.

"What are we doing here?" Max asked.

"Ditching the limo," Jared answered. "Let's go!"

Max decided not to question his brother's judgment.

They hurried to rush into three additional vehicles. Shatara and Esmeralda rode with Slim, Max and Shatina grabbed Buster and rode with Rambo, and Jared rode solo.

They arrived at Luke, Jared's medic's house less than five minutes later.

The guys carried an unconscious Buster inside and put him onto Luke's operating table.

Buster wasn't moving.

Shatara's hands were covered with blood, as were Sam's.

"Oh my God..." Sam fainted.

Shatina and Esmeralda comforted her when she came to, while Shatara stood silent in shock.

"Is he gonna make it?" Max was almost too afraid to ask, but he had to know.

Luke wore a grim expression. "I'll try my best but it doesn't look good. What the hell happened?"

Everyone grew silent as Jared gave him a blow-by-blow account.

Chapter 26

It took quite a while, but Luke finally got the bullet out. "We're making progress, but he needs a transfusion."

"A transfusion?" Jared and Rambo said in unison.

Luke nodded. "Yeah guys, he's lost too much blood. I'll do a test, but since this obviously isn't a real hospital, I don't have spare blood lying around."

Everyone considered what that meant, but Jared was the first to speak. "I'll do it." He held out his arm.

"Hold your horses, buddy," Luke said. "I'll need to test his blood first to see what type he has, then I need to make sure you're a match." Luke glanced around the room. "Any more volunteers, in case Jared's not a match?"

One by one, everyone agreed.

Luke took small samples of everyone's blood, then ran them through the tests simultaneously. When he was finished, he inspected each one carefully.

"Okay, it looks like there's only one match." He glanced around the room until his eyes rested on one person. "Shatara, is it? Did I pronounce that right?"

Shatara nodded. "Yes."

"You up for this?"

She nodded again, swallowed, then stepped forward. "What do I need to do?"

Luke pulled up a chair. "Sit here for me," he gestured, and she obeyed. "I'm going to need to hook the needle to your vein, run it through this bag, and run it into Buster's vein. That cool?"

Shatara nodded.

Luke licked his lips with apprehension. "But just so you know, this may not work."

Everyone contemplated the weight of his words while Shatara relaxed in the chair. Luke quickly found her vein, then Busters, then began the process.

The process took three hours, and by the end of it, Buster's vitals had returned to normal, but he slipped into a coma.

"Oh my God..." Sam said. "This night just keeps getting worse."

Shatara was weak from the transfusion. She threw up on the floor, and Luke tended to her by feeding her and giving her fluids.

No one wanted to leave Buster, so they decided to stay at Luke's spot for the night, praying that he would regain consciousness during the night.

The next morning, the city was in a frenzy, and Buster still hadn't woken up. The crew watched the news and learned that several men had been arrested at the club, while numerous other suspects were considered at large.

"We gotta lay low for a while," Jared said, then he yawned, as if this were an everyday occurrence.

Rambo looked unbothered as well, while Sam, Max, Shatina, and Shatara contemplated their options.

Esmeralda bore an expression of fear.

Chapter 27

After two days at Luke's spot, Buster still showed no signs of waking up. Luke called a meeting. He glanced at Buster, then Jared before he spoke. "Guys, I know we're holding out hope here, but we're running out of options. If he doesn't wake up soon, I'm going to run out of resources. We'll need to either take him to a hospital, maybe under a different identity, or let him go."

"We can't take him to a hospital!" Shatina said. "Brighton might figure out he's there."

"And what do you mean, let him go?" Shatara said, her eyes full of disgust.

Luke held his hands up. "Look, I'm just telling you the reality of the situation."

Everyone watched as Sam got up and stalked toward the door.

"Where are you going?" Max asked.

"Home," she said, and slammed it behind her.

The rest of the crew looked at each other.

"One of us should go after her," Max urged.

Jared shook his head. "No, let her go. I'm honestly tired of being cooped up here myself. We should all go home." He threw back the rest of the bag of chips he was munching on, then crumpled the bag and threw it into the trash bin.

"How are we all just going to go home?" Max asked. "They'll arrest us before we make it down the street."

Jared hopped off the counter he was sitting on, then eyed him. "Haven't you been watching the news, bro? They have no idea who we are. Remember, we were all wearing masks, plus we changed our appearance. Chill out, we're not gonna get caught."

"So what are we supposed to do, just leave him here?" Shatina said, gesturing toward Buster.

Rambo entered the room, holding a bottle of liquor. "I think we should have done this the other night, but there's no time like the present."

They watched as he opened the bottle, then tipped it, splashing some on Luke's pristine tile.

"Dude, that's my floor!"

Rambo shot him a sheepish grin. "Hey man, it's a special occasion. Seth was a rider, though he originally played for the other team."

"What do you mean, the other team?" Shatina asked.

Rambo and Jared shared a look, but neither of them said anything.

Shatara stared at each of them in disgust before she lost it. "Do you all hear yourselves? What is wrong with you!"

Chapter 28

Shatina had a feeling this was coming, but she had hoped her sister would let out her emotions when they got back home.

"All of you are crazy!" Shatara continued. "You're standing there, joking about a man who got his face blown off right in front of us. Not to mention Buster, who's laying there fighting for his life. You don't want to bring him to the hospital, and you're actually considering just letting him die?" Shatara turned to Shatina with incredulous rage. "Who are you?"

Those words stung, but Shatina understood her twin's anger.

"Shatara, everyone's stressed right now. Let's just..."

"No, I'll tell you who's stressed. Me!" Shatara pointed at herself. "I got kidnapped while walking back to my dorm on a random night, shoved into the back of a van, and almost sold off as a sex slave!"

Shatina could see the vein in her sister's left temple, she was so upset.

"And it was all your fault, Shatina," she spat. "All your voices and secret behavior, and you almost got me killed. You almost got all of us killed." She pointed at Shatina's chest as she spoke. "Seth is dead because of you. I hate you!"

Shatina stepped back, her body numb, but Max stepped in. "Shatara, you've got it all wrong. Shatina did everything she could to save you. She wanted nothing more than for you to be okay."

"Well why didn't she just turn herself in then?" Shatara retorted. "Brighton gave her the option when he recorded that video. Ever think of that, twin? Or at least calling the cops and telling them what happened? Of course not. And why? Because you were busy trying to save your own ass, not mine!"

Shatina didn't have any words to respond to her sister.

"Now I'm going home," Shatara announced. "You guys can go on and do whatever the hell you're going to do with Buster. I did everything I could to save him. His blood won't be on my hands."

"Wait," Esmeralda said, speaking for the first time since they entered Luke's spot.

Shatara froze on her way out and turned back to face her. "I'm sorry, Esmeralda. I appreciate everything you did for me in there, but I need to leave this place before I lose my mind."

"No," Esmeralda said, and reached out to grab her arm. "Please stay for me. I have nowhere to go. Can you at least wait until I have a plan?"

The rest of the crew watched in silence as Shatara contemplated Esmeralda's request.

Finally, her expression softened. "Okay, I'll stay a bit longer." She cut her eyes at Shatina. "But only for Esmeralda."

"Hey! We helped you too!" Jared joked, pointing to himself and Rambo, but Shatara didn't bother to respond.

Shatina was grateful that Esmeralda bought them some time, but she didn't know what she would do when Shatara decided to leave Luke's spot for good.

Chapter 29

Sam was spiraling, but she no longer cared. One hundred and forty three calls to Robert, and not one time did he answer.

She sat on her bathroom floor with a knife in one hand, and a positive pregnancy test in the other.

Her life was officially over, before it had a chance to begin.

The baby was Robert's, she knew that, but she never had a chance to tell him with everything that was looming over their heads.

She found out about the pregnancy when she first started experiencing symptoms while developing the plan with the crew, and she was going to tell him once things died down.

Now it seemed that there was no end in sight, and Sam couldn't take being in that house anymore.

None of them could possibly understand the situation she was in. Sam had no one. Her father wrote her off, her mother was hanging on by a thread with her depression, Max and Shatina had their own issues, Buster was in a coma, and Robert wasn't answering.

Sam stared at the knife as it glinted under the reflection of the light.

One or two swipes, and it would all be over.

She never thought she would face a day like this, and a small part of her was telling her she didn't have to give up now.

But how was she supposed to raise a child, when she could barely manage her own life?

What aspirations did she have outside of plotting and scheming?

The one good relationship she had, she ruined it.

Waited all that time for a good man, just to betray him.

She was no better than her father, no better than Brighton, no better than anyone.

There was no point in continuing the drama.

Sam sighed, flipped the pregnancy test onto the floor, then reached for her phone to see if Robert had called or texted back.

He hadn't.

Her phone was a ghost town, and she was about to be a ghost.

Sam's mind flashed to Shatina, Max, and the rest of the crew and contemplated whether she should stick around a bit longer to make sure they all turned out okay.

Then she shook her head, deciding against it. She was useless anyway.

The plan had barely worked, and now they were all facing serious charges if the police ever discovered their identities.

She was better off following through with this plan.

So she did.

After sending one last text to the crew, Sam lay on the floor, made herself comfortable, and swiped her left wrist, then her right.

Once that was over, she waited for darkness to claim her for good.

122

Chapter 30

The crew continued to watch the news throughout the day. So far, no updates as far as Brighton Miller, the girls, or possible identities of the suspects at large.

They had no way of knowing if the police had been alerted of their identities and just weren't releasing that information to the media, or if they had gotten away.

The truth was, even if they were undetected by law enforcement, their problems were far from over.

Brighton Miller was still out there, and it wouldn't take a genius to figure out who took Shatara.

Cops or not, they had targets on their back.

The pressure was insurmountable.

Shatina felt like she was about to crack.

Then the straw came that broke the camel's back.

Max received three calls from Ted, back to back. He wasn't going to answer at first, but Shatina urged him to. Maybe it was important.

Max answered with him on speaker. "Hello?"

"Hey Max, have you talked to Sam?"

Max looked confused for a second, then slowly gave his response. "Earlier... why?"

Ted sighed. "It's a long story, but we broke up the other day. She called me a bunch of times and I wasn't going to answer, but then she left me a strange voicemail."

Shatina's ears pricked up, and everyone's eyes shot toward Max's phone.

"What do you mean, a strange voicemail?"

Ted continued. "She was mostly rambling, but it was less about what she said, and more about the way she said it. I'm pulling up to her place now."

Shatina's heart pounded. Something felt wrong.

They heard movement as Ted must have been approaching Sam's door, then there were knocking sounds. "It's open," he commented, then they heard him shuffling through the house.

"Sam! Sam!" he called out.

More movement, and then, "Oh sh....!" He swore. "I'll call you right back."

The line went dead, and nervous tension filled the room.

Max stood. "We gotta go over there."

Shatina agreed.

"All of us can't go though," Jared said, looking serious for once.

Max and Shatina nodded and continued toward the door.

"Wait!" Esmeralda called out.

They turned back to face her, wondering what she wanted all of a sudden.

"Before you go," she started. "I need to tell you something."

"What is it?" Max asked. "We need to check on Sam."

"I know." Esmeralda looked uneasy. "I wanted to mention this earlier, but Brighton Miller has my sister. If I would have known you were coming for Shatara the other night I would have tried to get her out too. Everything happened so fast, but..." Her eyes clouded. "I need you to help me save her."

To be continued...

Dear Reader,

The saga continues. If the crew wasn't already in a dire predicament at the end of the last story, they sure are facing the fire now. Will Buster pull through, or is he lost forever? Is Sam already gone? Will Shatina and Shatara ever be able to repair their relationship? Finally, is there something brewing beneath the surface that the crew may not be ready for? Find out all of that and more in the jaw-dropping finale of the Quiet Ones Series, The Enemy You Know.

Until next time,

Tanisha Stewart

Before you go...

If you enjoyed *Surprise Surprise*, I would absolutely love to hear your feedback. Please leave a **rating** or **review** commenting on your overall thoughts.

In addition, if you would like access to exclusive updates, giveaways, and more, join my email list at tanishastewartauthor.com/contact.

God bless you, and happy reading!

Tanisha Stewart

PS: If you would like to connect with me on social media, here's where you can find me:

Facebook: Tanisha Stewart, Author
Facebook group: Tanisha Stewart Readers
Instagram: tanishastewart_author
TikTok: authortanishastewart
Twitter: TStewart_Author
YouTube: Tanisha Stewart

Tanisha Stewart's Books

Even Me Series
Even Me
Even Me, The Sequel
Even Me, Full Circle

When Things Go Series
When Things Go Left
When Things Get Real
When Things Go Right

For My Good Series
For My Good: The Prequel
For My Good: My Baby Daddy Ain't Ish
For My Good: I Waited, He Cheated
For My Good: Torn Between The Two
For My Good: You Broke My Trust
For My Good: Better or Worse
For My Good: Love and Respect
Rick and Sharmeka: A BWWM Romance

Betrayed Series
Betrayed By My So-Called Friend
Betrayed By My So-Called Friend, Part 2
Betrayed 3: Camaiyah's Redemption
Betrayed Series: Special Edition

Phate Series
Phate: An Enemies to Lovers Romance
Phate 2: An Enemies to Lovers Romance
Leisha & Manuel: Love After Pain

The Real Ones Series
Find You A Real One: A Friends to Lovers Romance
Find You A Real One 2: A Friends to Lovers Romance
Janie & E: Life Lessons

The Quiet Ones Series
Should Have Thought Twice: A Psychological Thriller
Fooled Me Once: A Psychological Thriller
Never Saw Me Coming: A Psychological Thriller
Reap What You Sow: A Psychological Thriller
Surprise Surprise: A Psychological Thriller
The Enemy You Know: A Psychological Thriller

Standalones
A Husband, A Boyfriend, & a Side Dude
In Love With My Uber Driver
You Left Me At The Altar
Where. Is. Haseem?! A Romantic-Suspense Comedy
Caught Up With The 'Rona: An Urban Sci-Fi Thriller
#DOLO: An Awkward, Non-Romantic Journey Through Singlehood
December 21st: An Urban Supernatural Suspense
Everybody Ain't Your Friend: An Urban Romance Thriller
The Maintenance Man: A Twisted Urban Love Triangle Thriller
Not What It Seems: A Christian Romance Thriller
Vengeance Is Mine: A Psychological Thriller